The Magical Train

By Aaron Alberto

Special thanks to the editors who helped me wordweave together this book, Jenifer Danielle and Cameron R..

Major props to Rela from Brazil for making the cover of this book, she truly brought to vision the wonders that were inside of my head.

Photograph credits to the lovely Donovan Costa, who made my summer nights special!

Love to my Fanon Wiki community, without you guys, I wouldn't even be here!

This book is dedicated to my family, friends, teachers and most importantly to anybody who is facing any sort of oppressive violence, may your endurance and strength lead you towards a path full of love and light. You are made out of star particles, and will shine no matter how much darkness surrounds you.

Sincerely, Aaron Alberto

Chapter 1:The Storm

A figure stood by the edge of the shore, taking a deep breath of the salty morning air, he looked out into the Caribbean sea where the dazzling morning rays began to light up the azure body of water. The landscape was glorious, the type to tenderly lift up a person's mood by the meer sight. Lautaro knew by heart that it was going to be a glorious morning and nothing was going to change that.

Throughout the month of July, Lautaro had decided to travel all over the Caribbean Sea; he flew from island to island. Having had the privilege of attending an aviation program during High School, he was able to complete the program and obtain his private pilot license by the youthful age of 19.

Presently, in his early 20's, it was his ambition to fly all around the world by plane, fulfilling his lifelong dream to become an aviator.

Wrapping up his final destination in the Caribbean, Lautaro had stayed on the canny, lovely island of Bonaire for his final day. Today, after sunrise, he was to head out and promptly return to the American states.

Before doing so, he went to the house of the local family that had hosted him for the night to heartily wish them all a fond farewell. It was a hospitable family of four: parents, daughter and grandmother. Smiling, he shook the hands and hugged them all, from the eldest to the youngest, making sure to show them all his sincere appreciation for their embracing welcome towards him. As Lautaro was about to leave, the grandmother politely handed him a silver chain necklace that contained Bonaire coins dangling from its end.

"Stay safe, young one," she told him, placing the necklace on the palm of his hand and enclosing it with her own. She gave him one last affectionate smile before turning and walking back to her family.

Lautaro instantly put the necklace around his neck, showing gratitude for the gift the grandmother had given him. He beamed at the local family and waved goodbye to them all, one last time, before heading out to where his airplane was stationed.

Upon boarding his plane, Lautaro instantly started the engine, as the front fins of the plane began to spiral, he cautiously started to steer the airplane forward until it started gaining momentum to be in the air. Once adrift, Lautaro flew away from the island and began navigating above the sea. He flew and he flew, feeling free like a bird as he did so. His flight was peaceful for half an hour, and Lautaro keenly enjoyed the view of the majestic landscapes that the Caribbean had to offer from an aerial view. The panorama gave him a sense of excitement and accomplishment causing him to drift into a daydream of sorts. At the moment, he felt at peace aviating over the West Indies, nothing else in life could compare. Not only was the weather favorable, it was the pure definition of serenity. Optimal flying conditions were present for that morning as the sky was clear and the sun was shining, but not blinding.

However, as Lautaro started nearing the Bermudan region, he began to notice a significant change in the weather as the once clear skies began churning with deep gray clouds. As he neared the apex center of the Bermuda Triangle, the harsh weather radically started altering to windy and stormy, the clouds rolled over one another which led to the underpowered engine of Lautaro's plane to start acting perilously. Now in midst of the fierce rain storm, his view fogged up, making it difficult to see where he was heading.

Fearing the worst case scenario, Lautaro immediately started to transmit emergency radio signals out to the aviation bases in Florida. He declared that he was caught up in a relentless storm within the Bermudan region and that he was unsure of the opportunity of making it back home. The odds did not seem in Lautaro's favor. "Tell my family and my wife-," his voice was shaking, starting to give out. He took a deep breath as he swiped the beads of sweat that were starting to form on his forehead. "Tell my family that I. . .I love them all so much," With a screech of static, Lautaro's radio gave out.

Just when he thought that things could not get any worse, a lightning bolt struck down the edge of one of his plane's wings, haltering it, and the plane started dwindling down, rotating dramatically as it started to free fall. Lautaro held on for life, for it was dear, if there was even a chance to get through this. As the plane hit the sea, the water became a whirlpool of sorts, taking in everything in its surroundings and swallowing it up. Lautaro, while alive and breathing, began to accept his cruel fate for the worst as the whirlpool continued to grow stronger. The pressure from the whirlpool was excruciating, and Lautaro knew he and his plane were not coming out of this in one piece. After being tossed around for what felt to be a lifetime, but was in fact only around a minute, Lautaro felt his eyes begin to get heavy. His heartbeat rocked inside his ears, pounding and pounding, his vision focused in and out, the ocean was getting darker, or was he just hallucinating? The roars of his plane, struggling to stay in one and the ocean's screeches were the last things Lautaro heard before everything went dark.

Coming to, Lautaro found himself gently laid on rocky, moist dirt. He reached his hand out to his forehead, which was slightly throbbing, and realized his hair was matted with a dark auburn substance. He decided he should get up, still trembling and at a pace slower than a turtle, Lautaro managed to prop himself up and tried to make sense of what precisely had happened. Once upon his feet, he looked all around and realized he had somehow ended up on the shore of a mild river stream, adding in to his confusion even more. His attention was immediately caught by a nearby arc bridge over the river; its mirroring reflection into the river created the illusion of a circular "O" shaped ring. Lautaro thought that it looked neat, as he instantly realized that near, under the bridge laid his airplane, with shattered windows, a missing wing, and torn up flying fins. While it was most definitely in a shabby state, Lautaro knew he could fix it within a contemporary time given the effective tools to do so.

Not possessing a clue on earth as to where he was, he decides to go take a look around to which he heard a sudden train engine come to a halt not too far away, and saw that a smoke trail in the sky. Curious to know if there were anyone on the train, he promptly decides to naturally go towards the specific direction of the smoke trail. Surrounded by exotic woods, he willingly entered them, instantly noticing the intriguing purple hue on the glossy leaves of the trees which were an autumn orange. He continued on walking in the rare woods until his chosen path started to clear up, which broadened the prevailing view.

There, he saw an express train made up of an articulated locomotive and five distinct sections. Sitting at ease on the edge of the locomotive, he noted a young woman with wavy, dark hair wearing a train conductor uniform with a hat, overalls and everything. She was contentedly munching on what appeared to correctly be a ham sandwich and stopped as promptly as she noticed Lautaro tentatively approaching.

"Woah, where did you come from," she politely asked him, startled to witness someone in such a rural area.

"Umm, the Caribbean Sea, I suppose," replied Lautaro back, not providing a satisfactory answer.

"I have never heard of such a place," justly said the woman unamused, thinking that Lautaro might not have good intentions as she allegedly started getting up and packing her sandwich away.

As for Lautaro, he assumed the woman was either not very bright or joking because to him it would seem that everyone has heard about the Caribbean unless they have lived the entirety of their lives under a rock.

"Could you at the very least tell me where I am," he allegedly asked her.

"You are in Alnidor, the land of rumpops," she said, "you do not suppose that I take you to my town as you seem lost!"

"Never heard of such a place," Lautaro said, "and yes, could you take me to the closest town, I need to get back home."

"Alrighty then, get'er on board," she said giggling, out of the blue, as she offered her hand out to him. Lautaro got closer to the train and her, he was about to willingly give her his hand but then he paused for a moment...he wondered if his plane would be alright if he left it alone? Surely it would still be there because after all, it appears that no one is in sight in these wooded areas. This possible doubt of secureness gave Lautaro enough confidence to reach his hand out to this mysterious woman, who he was unsure if he could trust.

However, seeing as she was the sole person around

who might willingly aid him he went with her.

This woman, who had an air of strangeness

to her, cheered as she generously helped Lautaro

climb on to the train. Now in the locomotive,

Lautaro watched as the woman started the train's

engine as the steam trumpet let out a "choo-choo",

and the train started to undoubtedly continue on the

path of the railroad track it was on.

The woman directed her considerable

attention to Lautaro who was timidly looking

around the locomotive, and complimented his

fashionable jacket, noting that it looks lavish.

"It is an aviator jacket," Lautaro proudly said, "I bought it from West Louis, after properly obtaining my pilot license!"

The likely woman thoughtfully nodded her head, properly acknowledging to have heard what he stated. "I do not think we have properly introduced ourselves," she remarked, "I correctly am Emerson."

"Well nice to meet you Emerson," Lautaro said, "I am Lautaro."

"Sounds like a bull's name to me," she said as she instantly started giggling before getting serious again, "Sorry, that is solely what entered my mind!"

"Say...," Lautaro said as he carefully looked around the locomotive, "Is there anywhere on the train for me to sit down?"

"Oh, yes, right, follow me," Emerson said as she opened the door with a spiral knob naturally leading to the rest of the express train.

Lautaro stepped into the following section of the train, he took his first glance of it and admired the way that the passengers' section of the train had small but decorative chandeliers, hanging from the trains' roof, which highlighted the mellow brown shades of the seats, and the entire compartments that communicated a welcoming feeling to them. It undoubtedly had a vintage vibe going for it.

He walked over to the nearest compartment, carefully opened the slider door, and took a seat in one of the couch seats.He traced the embroidery

with his fingers, entranced by the wavy, flowing

designs carefully stitched into the upholstery. He

looked out the train and saw an endless sea of

purplish-orange trees being passed by. Emerson sat

down in the seat across from him after putting the

train on auto-conduct mode.

"Could you tell me a bit more about where I

am," Lautaro asked her, "In what continent is

Alnidor in? Europe?"

"In Europe? Do not know where that is,

however, Alnidor is located in the inner

north-Eastern part of upper Duggerland, which is

part of the greater Pacificus continent," she

explained to him.

Highly confused about what she had just told him, Lautaro said, "That is a lot to take in, do you by any chance have a map or a phone with you."

"I do not recognize what a phone is, but I do have a map with me," Emerson said as she went to the locomotive and returned some minutes later with a map, laying it out on the table that stood firmly between where she and Lautaro were seated.

Lautaro looked over at the map, he noted it looked somewhat similar to earth, but some of the water bodies and continents had been highly altered. Something about this map stood out to Lautaro as it took him a minute to realize it was an inverted version of planet earth.

"Woah, I do not remember the earth looking like this," he thought to himself.

"Is this a joke," he asked Emerson," Or did the earth change?"

"Most definitely not," replied Emerson, "it has habitually been like this except within its developmental stages."

"In that case, I must be on a completely different planet," said Lautaro as he slumped down in his seat, "or I am within some dream too real to escape."

"Right," said Emerson, highly confused before inevitably asking him, "What do you mean?".

Lautaro next began explaining his fascinating story, "You see, I am a private pilot, I fly around the world. However while flying in the Bermudan region, I was caught up in a storm and knocked out, when I awoke I ended up in this world -your world - it is altogether different from mine."

After hearing him say this, Emerson could only conclude that he was completely lost from reality.

"Well that is bizarre sounding," Emerson said, "I like to keep an open mind, but I am not quite sure if I believe you."

Wanting to instantly change the topic, she looked down on her watch and exclaimed, "Oh my sign, I am going to be late for the concert!"

"What concert," Lautaro asked as he leaned

over to take a brief glimpse at her watch. He noticed

that instead of numbers, it depicted some sort of star

signs or constellations.

"I don't think that it's your kind of thing,"

Emerson warily explained, "It is a protest concert."

"It sounds kinda rad," said Lautaro, eager to

hear more.

"I am going to bring a friend along," said

Emerson.

"Who," Lautaro asked her.

"You will see," she said as she gracefully

stood from her seat. She then proceeded to tell

Lautaro to feel free to look around the

compartment, as she headed out to conduct the

train's locomotive once again.

Heeding her advice, Lautaro began to look around. He looked out the window with cautious wonder. The sun was starting to fade away into an orange and lavender sunset as the dark hue of night started to take over. The chandeliers of the train illuminated his surroundings in a warm, amber hue. After some minutes of sitting alone, Lautaro noticed that the train had started slowing down, finally screeching to a halt. He clumsily moved from the compartment he was in into the one across from him to peer out through the window. There he saw a small log cabin amidst the woods.

He next heard the door leading to the locomotive open and heard Emerson yell out "Let us go meet my friend!"

Chapter 2:Rock and Roll

As soon as Lautaro and Emerson had gotten off the train, they promptly began walking down a small, grassy slope to undoubtedly reach the cabin. It seemed petite in standard width, enough space for one person to live in it. However it was tall, for a large person to inhabit it. The humble cabin had a floral wreath hanging from its front door, which naturally gave it a spring season theme.

Emerson started knocking on the door, it did not take many knocks for her to receive a response as the door began to start opening. A long-legged, burly man came out, closing the door behind him. This man had the appearance of a lumberjack with a bushy beard that bore flowers on it. He ordinarily wore sleeveless patterned prints, darks fitting pants, and some boots.

Emerson hugged him as she introduced him to Lautaro as her friend.

"Lautaro this is Budder, and Budder this is Lautaro," she told them.

"Oh man, that is an awesome jacket you got there," Budder exclaimed to Lautaro before asking him if he is attending the concert too.

"Thanks, and I do not think I am," Lautaro replied before shifting the subject by asking him, "did you put those flowers on yourself?"

"Umm no, they are natural," said Budder with a slight tone of offense.

Emerson noting the social awkwardness of Lautaro's innocent intentions behind his question chimed in to explain Budder's situation, "He is a flower man, usually women get this trait, and it is a rare genetic condition where people grow flowers in their hairs."

Lautaro was astounded by this unusualness and did not know if such odd things are possible, however, he briefly stated "Fascinating," as his mind examined the confusion about the situation he was in.

"Where am I again," he asked the duo of friends.

"In Alnidor, the lone land that makes quality rumpops," Budder said.

"Yup, that is right," Emerson chimed in.

"Huh, that is strange, so strange," said Lautaro "Nothing has been making sense."

"Oh, it never does," said Budder laughing as he erroneously thought that Lautaro must have been joking.

Lautaro did not think that he could handle any more maddening scenarios. He shouted, "I need to get back to my plane and get back home!"

Emerson, noting the change in Lautaro's attitude, sternly informed him, "Hold up now, my friend, you are on my transportation and I am late for an important concert, that is where we are going next."

Not wanting to reasonably argue with her, Lautaro simply said, "Alright, let us go, but after the concert, you are taking me back to my plane, deal?!"

"Sounds like an exceptional deal to me," Emerson said as she crossed her arms.

"Well, what are we delaying for? Let us go party!" Budder exclaimed.

Emerson, who had been staring thoughtfully at Lautaro with a sour look on her face, nodded her head slightly to the side, pointing at her express train, signaling for him to go with them. The trio then soon began to walk up the slight, grassy slope towards the train, getting on board of it.

Once Emerson had started the train's locomotive engine to typically induce it going on auto-conduct mode, she headed towards the train's sections that were in the end, leaving Lautaro and Budder to themselves in the compartment where they were seated.

"So what is this musical concert about," Lautaro politely asked Budder.

"It is a rock concert," Budder explained to him, "A protest concert to be exact."

"Well, what makes this organized protest so important," Lautaro asked him.

"It is a massive protest, we are protesting earnestly to the king for wanting to isolate the kingdom," Budder told him, "Some of our friends are in a band, so we are also going to support them."

"Ah, I see what is going on presently," said Lautaro, "Still I have to get back home."

"Where are you from," Budder asked him.

"Not from here, that is for sure," said Lautaro, not wanting to reveal a lot about himself to a someone he had barely met.

Just then Emerson came into the compartment where they were, "Hey there, who is ready to rock and roll," she said, having changed out into her party outfit.

"That is a wicked look there, Em," Budder complimented her, "I like the top hat and goggles."

"Much appreciated, Budder," she said as she took a seat next to Lautaro.

"Are you excited about the concert," she asked Lautaro.

He merely shrugged and replied, "I guess so, I still do not perceive what the tremendous fuss about it is."

"It is a protest concert," Emerson continued to explain, "To show alliance within the nation as our king thinks it is keen to seclude the kingdom from the rest of the world."

"Well, why is he achieving that," asked Lautaro, "there must be a reason for it?"

"You sure ask many questions, do you not," Emerson told him.

"He thinks our nation is self-sufficient," Budder chimed in to say, "that we do not require anyone else's help, he is also engulfed in riches while money is starting to become more sacred for the rest of us."

The mention of money instantly made Lautaro fondly remember the coin necklace that the doting grandmother at Bonaire had given him. He gently touched upon his neck and looked down and realized it was no longer on him.

"Oh no," he justly said.

"What is wrong," Emerson asked him, noticing his profound dismay.

"Nothing," he immediately replied as he realized that his necklace must have been lost during the midst of the storm, upsetting himself. He did not want to express his heartfelt sorrow, so he just smiled at Budder and Emerson, saying, "Everything is fine."

"I right now see what is wrong about the King's rule," he told them.

The express train then came to a stop.

"Well guys, we are here," said Emerson. One, by one they left the compartment and headed out of the train via the locomotive slider doors. Emerson made sure to lock up the train securely with her keys and place a wooden board over the slider door. By now it was nighttime, Lautaro looked up at the moonlit sky to observe two full moons that appeared to be within opposite sides of each other. One was of the color blue, while the other one was of the color pink, together they caused a faint light over the cultivated land of a colored purple hue.

"Wow, that is gorgeous," said Lautaro.

"It sure is," stated Emerson as she handed him a lantern to illuminate his way, "Now let us keep moving."

"Towards where do we go," Lautaro asked and then said, "There are no paths in here, just wooded areas."

"Exactly," said Emerson, "Through the forest we go until we come across the path." She started leading the way towards the woods, as Lautaro and Budder followed behind her.

Once they were walking in the midst of the woods, Lautaro could not help but feel terribly a slight nervousness at the unusual sight of the crooked trees. The bark on them appeared to have sculpted the odd shape of angry faces on them over time and lacked any leaves. He suddenly heard overhanging branches breaking off as something glided through them. He ran frantically to hug Budder in horrible fear.

"I perceived something in the trees," he exclaimed.

"It is most likely just a bird," Emerson said, "Now let us keep moving."

"Yeah, just calm down and faithfully keep moving, we are practically there," said Budder as he gently pushed off Lautaro from himself.

To experience a more pleasing sense of safety, he decided to walk in between Budder and Emerson, feeling less exposed to any possible dangers he imagined of the woods. They kept walking until soon loud blaring music could be heard in the distance that only got more clear as they got close to it. They kept walking and soon they saw jars of lights hanging from trees, their entrance from the sombre forest intersected with the lighted path leading up to where the concert is.

"Why did we not follow to walk from the path right from the start," Lautaro inquired Emerson.

"Because you never know what can happen in these kinds of concerts," she explained, "They are risky and I have to keep my train hidden."

They promptly started walking on the dirt path, lighted by clear jars of lights hanging from the trees, entering the wide landmass out in the open where the concert took place. It was blaring with loud rock music, and hundreds of people were in attendance at the concert! Everyone present was dressed to the nines, wearing festive and colorful outfits, along with decorative face paint.

As Lautaro, Emerson, and Budder gathered around the crowd, Lautaro was suddenly approached by a man yelling out loudly "rumpops, rumpops, get one free, elaborate courtesy of the community!"

He was stunned by this unannounced man appearing as Emerson enthusiastically encouraged him to get a rumpop from the tray that the man was carrying, "try one, they are absolutely good!"

Lautaro reached out to grab a rumpop from the loaded tray that the man was holding. He grabbed for the pop that was shaped like a golden star and delivered it a bite, and to his surprise, it was exceptionally good! It tasted like rum-flavored cake with an extraordinary delicacy of eggnog. He thought it was pleasant, but with some milk would be even more enjoyable.

"Do you like it," Budder asked him.

"I most definitely do," yelled out Lautaro as he reached towards the tray with his hands to grab some more rumpops, which some were shaped like stars, while others like planets that were unfamiliar to him.

Emerson and Budder started to dance near the crowd as a band was playing loud energetic, rock music that possessed a touch of the violin in it. Lautaro merely stood watching from the sides, as he ate the handful of rumpops he had with himself, enjoying the moment of serene festivity that was in front of him.

When the band that was playing completed their song, they headed out of the stage as a presenter took over the microphone to give out a speech over the purpose of the concert.

"Ladies and gents," the presenter yelled out into the microphone.

"Thank you all for attending this concert, it is a blast to party, dancing itself exhibits a sense of freedom," the presenter continued speaking to switch to a more serious topic," as you know the King, King Hansen has declared the kingdom to enter isolation as we are self-sufficient according to him."

"What is wrong with that," Lautaro asked as Emerson overheard him and gave him a hard stare before telling him "Just listen and you will see what is wrong with all that is going!"

Lautaro still could not make sense of what was going on around, yet he decided not to express his mind further as he felt quite uneducated on the topic of Alnidor's bureaucratic matters.

The presenter on the stage subsequently went on saying, "With isolation comes a lack of the exterior, without it, there can not be any evolution of ideas and enlightenment, everything remains stale, which would perhaps be fine if stable, but that affects our economy with a minor reduction of trade and the King appears to be hoarding the majority of the wealth now and do we want that?!"

"NOOOO," the frenzied crowd roared loudly.

Bored to be standing still for a long time and hearing the discourse, Budder promptly decides to inquire Emerson by whispering in her ear, "Hey Em, do you think we can go backstage and see our friends? It is not for nothing, but it is crowded out here."

"You know that is a clever idea," Emerson whispered back to Budder as she shouldered Lautaro to capture his personal attention and inform him to come with her and Budder.

The presenter who had been talking for a while now went on declaring, "With this shift of governing ambiance, I ask for all of you to please utilize your voices to make it clear to King Hansen that we do not want to isolate ourselves from the rest of the world!"

Lautaro, Emerson, and Budder walked around the crowd to reach the backstage.

There they were met by an armed security personnel who stood there with a sword, obstructing them from reaching the backstage stairs that lead to the back of the stage.

As he saw them approaching, he asked them for their reason for arrival.

"We have friends here, now let us pass," Emerson said as she valiantly attempted to walk past the security guard.

"Nobody is allowed without a pass, sorry," said the security guard.

Angry by hearing this, but trying to show a calm demeanor Emerson merely said, "That is ridiculous, and well then tell the gallant band of The Shapes to come to get us!"

"I can not do that; I am to stay here until the concert is over," the security guard went on to say, "now leave or you guys will face the consequences

of being trespassers!"

Emerson, while frustrated could only say

"You sure are stubborn, but I guess we will go then,

no need to discuss with a dimwit."

Bitterly disappointed, she along with

Lautaro and Budder turned around to start leaving.

However unexpectedly they all turned back

around when they heard someone call out for them,

"Hold on, wait you guys, I am coming!"

Lautaro saw a young man, with moderately

long hair, wearing a bandana, and rock star-like

attire coming, running down the stairs.

"Kearu," yelled out Emerson in excitement

as she ran towards him to give him a huge,

embracing hug.

The security guard was stunned by Kearu's sudden appearance and asked him, "Do you recognize who any of these people are?"

"Yes dear sir, these people are my friends," replied Kearu as he stopped to take a look at Lautaro with an amiable smile, "Except for this one, however, he can be my new friend."

This sort of notice traditionally made Lautaro feel welcomed and cherished, knowing he was part and included in this group of people's social circle. The security guard then allowed Emerson, Lautaro and Budder to accompany Kearu up backstage. "Off you go," he told them.

"Definitely, that is more like it," Emerson said snarkily.

The group started walking on the large stairs that led up to the backstage of the stage. "So when are you guys going to play," Emerson asked Kearu as the group walked up the stairs to the backstage.

"We are going up next," Kearu replied, "after the presenter is done giving his speech, so unfortunately I do not have much time to talk with you guys."

"Holy cow, that presenter sure loves communicating a lot," exclaimed Budder.

Once backstage, Kearu led the group to a portable room that was individually made for him and his bandmates. "After all of you," said Kearu as he held the door open for the trio of friends to enter. Lautaro was the first of the group to enter the room which he immediately noted to be filled with glamorous decor and furniture. Upon his arrival, he was greeted by two other guys that were at present in the room to which he assumed were his Kearu's bandmates.

"Eagerly welcome all of you," said one of the official band members, "take a seat wherever you would like to!"

As Lautaro sat down on one of the plush couches in the room which was soft, and embroidered with small, decorative moon holographic confetti, he was properly introduced to the other two band members, as Emerson and Budder joined in and sat next to him.

"This is Diamien," Kearu told Lautaro as he correctly pointed to the band member with the fringes.

"Oh hello there, I admire your hair," Lautaro told him.

"Thank you, I receive that a lot," he said to him before asking him," and what is your name?"

"Well, my proper name is Lautaro," Lautaro replied back ,"Lautaro Vacas."

"I do not recognize why, but your name makes me think of a bull," Diamien said.

"Yes, I get that a lot," said Lautaro.

Kearu then introduced Lautaro to the other band members. He was seated next to Diamien ," and over there is Sicur," pointing at him, Sicur, who had slicked back, platinum blonde hair.

"Hey there," Lautaro told him as he gave him a slight hello wave.

"Sup," said Sicur , "nice meetin' ya!" He then reached out to the center table and grabbed a teapot that was shaped like a whole lettuce and asked Lautaro along with his friends if they would like some blueberry tea.

"Sure," replied Lautaro as Sicur reached out to seize a cup that was shaped like a flower from the table, and poured some tea into it before delivering it to him. He did the same for Budder who gladly accepted it, and then to Emerson who politely declined.

Kearu sat down on the couch where his longtime bandmates were which was opposite of the couch where Lautaro and his friends were sitting. "So Emerson, how did you, and your unknown friend meet," he asked her.

Lautaro meanwhile took a sip of the tea from the flower-shaped cup that he was holding, he found it to be delicious, retaining a warm, fruity flavor to it. "Wow, this is extremely good," said Lautaro.

"He exactly came out of nowhere," Emerson exclaimed as she leaned over to take a look at Lautaro who was gulping down on his cup of tea.

Once he was done consuming his tea, Lautaro said "Well actually I am not that random!"

"Nothing wrong with being random," said Diamien as he chimed in to say, "at least if it is not as accidental as Sicur's mood swings!"

Sicur got extremely inflamed and erroneously called him out by saying, "Shut up, we all know you are not a good drum player as you think you are, those hand movements of yours- they are truly random at times!"

Kearu immediately stepped in to calm his bandmates as they were going up to play music next on stage and knew they would have to be within a pleasant frame of mind to play professionally.

"Settle down you guys. We are about to play next, now is no time to be fighting," Kearu said, trying to tranquil his band peers down," Anywho, how has your family been, Emerson?"

"They are doing great," Emerson then went on to say, "They think I should not be protesting against the kingdom but still give me a free will."

Feeling that the conversation that was being held had shifted out of his range of topics, Lautaro did not care to join in on the discussion with the group. He got up from his seat and started heading

out.

No one initially noticed Lautaro leaving

except for Kearu. "Hey where are you going, Lau,"

he asked him.

Startled to have realized that Kearu noticed

him leaving, he merely told him and the rest of the

group, including his friends, "It is a bit too tight

spaced here for me, I am going out to get some

fresh air and also keep an eye on the lanterns we left

dangling in the tree, to make sure no one stole

them."

He then proceeded to gently open the door

of the portable room in which he was in, and before

he stepped out Emerson informed him, "Hey

Lautaro, we will catch up to you, and remember to

be safe and if you have trouble finding us then just stay by our hang out spot or return to the train."

"I got it, thank you," Lautaro replied to her.

Lautaro then thanked her and everyone else in the room for the generous hospitality as he exited the portable room, closing its door behind him, he started walking towards the stairs to start heading out of the backstage.

Chapter 3:Ambush Ahead

Lautaro began to walk down the stairs to leave the backstage, and head out into the field where all the concert attendees were partying and dancing. He was greeted by the security guard with a slight nod of acknowledgment as he walked past by him.

As he started to turn the corner of the stage's ground holdings to head towards where the crowd is, he unexpectedly bumped into someone hard, making both himself and the other person fall to the ground.

"Ouch, that hurt, could you be a bit more careful when walking," stated Lautaro as he groaned in pain, rubbing his forehead.

"I, I am sorry," said the person as he stood up to give his hand out to Lautaro. Lautaro reached out his hand for his and got up, as the stranger pulled him up on his feet.

Lautaro let out small groans to indicate his pain, before saying "Thank you, and well I got to keep on moving."

The stranger, now curious to know about Lautaro, immediately asked him "Wait, how come I have never seen you around here before, are you new around here?"

"Yes, in a way, I am," said Lautaro as he started to walk onward on his way to his hang out spot. The stranger then ran up to him to halt him in his tracks, startling Lautaro, "wait I have not introduced myself yet, I am Sabriel."

"Uh that is cool," said Lautaro nervously as he quickly started to think of a conversation starter to have with Sabriel who he had just met, he took notice of his dark brown hair which was styled in that of a crew cut. "Are you enjoying the concert," he asked him.

"I am genuinely enjoying the concert very much, it is extremely neat, do you mind if we hang out," Sabriel asked Lautaro.

"Uh not at all," said Lautaro trying to be kind and pondering why an unknown stranger he had just met was taking so much interest in him so suddenly.

He and Sabriel started walking together around the edges of the large, partying crowd to reach his hang out spot which was near the trees where he and his new-made friends, Emerson and Budder had left their lanterns dangling from. Once, he and Sabriel were at ease, leaning against the trees, Lautaro looked up at the stage and realized that Kearu, and his bandmates, Sicur and Diamien were setting up their musical instruments to get ready to start performing some music.

"Oh this band is great," exclaimed Sabriel as he put his full attention to the stage, "The Shapes can really hype up a crowd!"

Having nothing else to do, Lautaro did the same, putting all of his attention on stage. Shortly after Kearu and his band (The Shapes) started playing a rock song with strong guitar riffs, Lautaro actually decided to loosen up after having been reserved for the entirety of his time in this strange, unusual world that he had landed upon and started to dance. Sabriel noticed this and started to cheer him on, particularly at Lautaro's swagger.

As Lautaro was dancing, jumping up and down excitedly as if no one was watching, Emerson and Budder arrived, they were both really surprised to see him in such a hyper mode. Emerson never expected to see Lautaro doing such a thing that she started laughing momentarily for such an out of the blue moment.

"Hey there, Lautaro," she called out to him, gaining his attention, "nice moves you got there!"

Lautaro got flustered as he did not realize how hyper he was when he was dancing within the moment, much to his friends' entertainment.

Budder noticed Sabriel leaning against the tree where their lanterns were hanging from and asked him, "Who are you?"

"Oh me," asked Sabriel, surprised to which he then said, "I am a friend of Lautaro."

"Lautaro, I did not know you possessed other friends," Budder turned to tell him.

Extremely busy dancing, Lautaro merely said jokingly, "Yes, I guess I am genuinely popular or whatever."

He undoubtedly continued dancing until The Shapes finished performing their first song.

"Alright you guys," announced Kearu into the microphone," for this next song, I want everyone to partner up with someone you appreciate as in you truly love them, any kind of love whether it be romantic, or friendly!"

Kearu then got off his microphone and turned around as he gripped firm on his guitar and told his band peers, "Hit it, fellas! And a one, a one, a one, two, three!"

Kearu then turned back around once again,

facing his focused attention to the crowd, he flicked

his fingers and suddenly pink, heart-shaped sparks

began to rain upon the crowd, as The Shapes began

to play a mid-tempo love, rock song.

Emerson grabbed a hold of Budder, "let us

dance, you are my best friend and for that, I will

always love you!" She and Budder walked over to

where the partying crowd were and started to slow

dance together as were most people at the concert.

Lautaro was hanging by the trees, along with

Sabriel, feeling a bit left out. "Do you want to

dance," Sabriel suddenly asked him."Uh sure, I

guess," said Lautaro, "Why not?!"

The two then started walking over to where

the crowd was and started slow dancing together

nearby where Emerson and Budder were dancing.

"What would you say our relationship is," Sabriel asked Lautaro."A friendship, I would assume," said Lautaro, as he and Sabriel slow danced, he decided to enjoy the music, and indulge in the atmospheric dance.

"The fact we have gotten close so fast could mean more," Sabriel told him.

Lautaro pondered at this statement made by Sabriel as to what brought them together so fast, however, the two continued on dancing together until The Shapes finished playing their love song.

"Alright you guys, this next one is for the freedom of people," yelled out Kearu into the microphone "hit it, you guys!"

Lautaro and Sabriel began to walk back to their hang out spot, as Emerson and Budder soon joined them as well.

The song that The Shapes started playing was one of a heavier sound, but really catchy, Lautaro was enjoying the music so much that he started head-banging his head. Emerson giggled surprised at Lautaro's current energetic manner. She too started to bobble her head along to the rhythm of the music, and eventually, Budder started doing the same as well.

As Kearu was playing his guitar, and singing into the microphone in midst of the song playing, flying sparks of light orbs of the color blue started to circulate and spiral in rotation all around him. When Lautaro saw this, he stopped his hysteric dancing and gasped in ultimate allure, not believing what he was witnessing.

"Woah," he shouted, "Are those real, or is it just stage effects?!"

Emerson in the midst of dancing and the loud music being played, yelled out to him over all the loud sound, "Yes they are real! He is a star soul!"

Curious to know what a star soul is, Lautaro yelled at her, "What is a star soul?!"

"They are highly gifted, intuitive individuals who are reigned by the stars," she yelled out to him, "some are born and some are made!"

Delighted and enlightened by all this new, mystical information, Lautaro simply exclaimed really out loud, "That is all really cool!"

As The Shapes were finishing their third song, Sabriel noticed a sound coming from the woods surrounding them, kind of like a large clumping down of the trees and/or twigs.

He quickly notified Emerson, Budder, and Lautaro about the sounds he was hearing emerging from the woods, putting a stop to their excitable dancing.

"I think that we should get out of here immediately," he told them frantically, "Something huge, and unexpected is coming towards us!"

"Wait, calm down, Sabriel, what exactly do you mean," Emerson asked him.

Sabriel proceeded to look Emerson straight into her eyes, and told her, "They have found us!"

He pointed at the woods, as the noise of breaking branches started to get louder! Emerson then looked at Budder in fear who looked back at her with a similar expression of alarm.

She walked over to Lautaro and grabbed him by the hand, pulling him, "Come on, let us go now, we are in danger," she remarked at him.

"What is going on," Lautaro asked her, showing both fright and confusion, as they sped walked around the crowd along with Budder and Sabriel to head towards the backstage.

"There is no time for me to answer now, I will explain everything to you later," Emerson yelled out at him, leading him towards the way.

"There is a secret tunnel in the backstage," she said.

Lautaro at this moment had entered into panic mode, however, he knew that if he wanted to be in a state of well being, he would have to listen to everything that Emerson tells him to do as he definitely sensed that she is the kind of person to help others when they are in need.

Lautaro, Emerson, Budder, and Sabriel all started running towards the backstage. The security guard ordered them to stop, however, they ignored his commands and ran right through him.

"Hey come back here," he angrily yelled at them, but they ignored him and just continued onto their way angering him to start cursing at them.

Meanwhile, on the stage, Kearu and his bandmates were getting ready to start playing another song but having a higher view on the stage of the open field and wooded area, he started to

sense that something was wrong, so he felt the need

to immediately start warning concert attendees

about it.

"Sorry to disrupt the party," Kearu yelled

into the microphone "but everyone run for your

lives, we are under attack!"

The crowd was momentarily confused by

this statement as Kearu and his bandmates let go of

their instruments and started running backstage, but

the crowd came to their senses of what was going

on when the trees surrounding the concert suddenly

came crashing down.

Knights in shiny silver armor wielding large

swords and armories came ready to destroy all that

was in sight. People started running in all directions,

scared for their lives, as some were slaughtered by the knights' sharp swords while others barely managed to escape, running into the woods, and hoping to see the end of the other side of them. The knights then started setting the field on fire, entrapping some of the concert attendees to meet their demise by being burned alive. Screams of sorrow, pain, and death were heard in all directions. Kearu and his bandmates, Diamien and Sicur went backstage where they met Lautaro, Emerson, Budder, and Sabriel. They heard all the commotion going on about within the open field, and knowing that people were being actively killed out there sent a cold shiver down Lautaro's spine as he felt a great amount of horror he had never felt before.

Kearu immediately led the way for them to his band's portable room. Once they were all in the room, he was quick to lock the door behind him. At the same time, outside a group of knights were heading towards the stairs that lead backstage. The security guard pulled out his sword ready to fight off the knights, to attempt to stop them from going to the stage.

He ran furiously towards one of the armed knights, yelling out, "get ready to inevitably feel the defeat!"

Just as he was going to bring his sword down upon one of the knights, he was pierced by another knight who went around, up behind him.

He was unfortunately outnumbered and had no armor to wear to fortify himself, so the security man at the concert was hacked to death by a hundred cuts of the knight men's lethal swords. His screams of unbearable agony were heard by Lautaro and his friends, along with The Shapes.

This forced Kearu into fast action to reveal where the secret tunnel was as he pushed the striped, colorful rug in the room that was covering it to the side with his foot. He quickly started to unlatch it, opening the passage towards the hidden tunnel. All who were present in the room started climbing down the ladder that led into the tunnel. Once Lautaro got in the tunnel which was circular in form and made up of moist dirt as it was underground, he was told by Emerson to keep running until they reached the end of the tunnel, so he did just that. He ran, and having previously done

Track and Field in high school, he was faster than

all those who were with him except for Sabriel who

was running at a speed faster than him, which made

him wonder if he had prior experience in some sort

of running based discipline.

Once they reached the end of the tunnel,

there was an opening that was covered by leaves

and tree branches on the edge of the trunk of a tree.

It led out into the other end of the woods where

Emerson had left her train.

As Lautaro helped her out of the tunnel she

told him," and this is why I chose not to take the

traditional path into the concert!"

It was extremely dark, only a dim purple

glow of the combined moons of different colors;

pink and blue illuminated the night. Emerson

headed over to her train, and pulled out her

collection of keys, she was having difficulty

searching for the key to open the locomotive's slider

door after she had unbarred it. While she was

searching for the right key, Lautaro noticed a small

trail of smoke coming from a distance away. He

realized that it was coming from the fire that the

knights had set aflame into the field of the concert.

While the night was beautifully dark

surrounded by mystic trees, standing on a small

grassy slope, and two beautiful colorful moons in

the sky, Lautaro felt a high sense of dread as the

smell of the fire smoke grew stronger.

"Need some help," Kearu asked Emerson as

his entire body started to glow up, he walked over

to where she was, lighting up her sight, making it

easier for her to find the key that she was looking
for.

"Aha, found it, yes thank you very much,"
she told Kearu as she excitedly found the key
pertaining to the locomotive door's lock, finally
being able to open.

"Finally," exclaimed Diamien, "because this
entire ordeal that just occurred was highly IFFY!"

They all started to laugh at the theatrical
way that Diamien had explained the situation.

"You can call it that for sure," Kearu said,
giving his friend a goofy smile.

Once Emerson opened the locomotive's
slider door, she, and her friends all hopped on board
of the train. Everyone was extremely tired, and as
they headed towards the compartment, they began

to either rest or take a nap, except for Lautaro who confronted Emerson about the deal they had previously made, while she was turning on the train's engine. "You need to take me back to where my plane is," he exclaimed to her, "all of this has been more than I bargained for!"

Emerson being tired after a long day of traveling and partying thought that it would be more rational for them to go see Lautaro's plane in the morning, but seeing how frantic he was and how he is basically homeless, she decided to take him back to where his plane was at after all this was part of the deal they had made.

"Alright, alright," Emerson said, as she headed to the locomotive to change the train's route on the railroad tracks, "That will be our next stop."

"Thank you," said Lautaro, now as he started to get a sense of ease for the first time in a while after having been filled with complete dread for some time now. He walked over to the train's following section and into the compartment where The Shapes along with Sabriel and Budder were seated at.

The band members must have all been extremely tired because they were all napping, while Budder and Sabriel sat in the opposite lounge couch seat from them, who Lautaro sat next to.

"Hey what were you and Emerson talking about," Budder sheepishly asked him?"

"We are to go see my plane," he told him.

"At this time, in the middle of the night," Budder replied, "I know a lot just happened, but we are all in danger under King Hansen's rule."

"That does not really matter to me," Lautaro said while shaking his head, "I just want to get back to my home."

"I see...," said Budder as he turned to look out the window.

The train then came to a halt, as Emerson announced through the train's radio speakers, "Lautaro if you come, we have arrived here!"

This loudness of the announcement startled The Shapes as they began to awake, "Woah, Woah," said Diamien, "Where are we?"

"In the woods still," replied Budder unamused.

"I might not come back after this," Lautaro told them as he got up from his seat to exit the compartment," so it has been good and see ya guys!"

He immediately rushed to go meet Emerson, who was waiting for him with her arms crossed, "Finally you are here," she said as she then started to open the locomotive's slider door. She grabbed a lantern from a hidden bin that was in the locomotive while Lautaro hopped off the train. He was not patient enough to wait for her to get the lantern, so he started rushing into the woods.

"Hey, wait up," Emerson yelled at him as she hopped off the train and hurried to catch up to him, "You might get lost!"

As Lautaro ran past the trees whose leaves were dominated by the color purple due to the two moon's combined glow, covering the land, as Emerson followed close behind him, their view was slowly broadened as they approached the river where Lautaro's plane had been left.

Once he got to the shore of the river, standing on the moist, rocky, sand, he looked all around for his plane, and much to his dismay it was nowhere to be found. He then ran to get closer to the circular arc bridge, but it was not there either! "No, no, no, this can not be," Lautaro exclaimed, "I swear my plane was right under this arc bridge!"

He was starting to tear and let out an exhausted wail as he fell to his knees, Emerson went up to give him a hug to try to comfort him.

"Listen, Lau, if I had to guess what happened, the knights were probably ordered by the King to take your plane to his castle," she told him.

"And now why would they do that, that is my plane," Lautaro exclaimed while in the midst of tears.

"Probably for investigative reasons," Emerson said, "they like to wrap a pretty bow on any wrong-doing that they do!"

"Yes, that is most likely and definitely what occurred," said Sabriel as he started to emerge from the trees.

"What are you doing here," Emerson asked him.

"You guys were taking a long time so I just wanted to see if everything is fine," said Sabriel as he shrugged, walking over to where they were.

"I think that if you go to the king and ask him politely then he might give you your plane back," he told Lautaro.

Lautaro then stopped tearing up, as he wiped his tears with his hands to get up to his feet, along with Emerson.

He looked at Sabriel skeptically, but in his mind at this point was willing to consider doing anything he could to retain his plane back.

"And how would that work exactly," Emerson asked Sabriel, "I do not believe the king is that kind of man."

"Do not worry, I will explain everything once we get back to the train," he said, "Come on let us go."

He started walking back to the woods, as Emerson and Lautaro looked at each other.

"It might be worth a try," Lautaro told her as he galloped, following Sabriel behind.

Emerson let out a loud sigh and then proceeded to run up to catch up to them, lighting up the way with her lantern in the dark woods until they reached the grassy slope that led up to the railroad track where her train was currently stationed.

The rest of their friends were waiting for them, as they were sitting on the ridge of the locomotive. As they saw Sabriel, Lautaro, and

Emerson coming out of the woods, they started

helping them hop on board of the train.

Chapter 4:Pale Shelter

While Emerson introduced the train

locomotive's engine on, Lautaro and the rest of the

guys went to take a seat in one of the compartments;

it was nighttime, so the chandeliers' lights warmed

the entirety of the train, conveying it a sense of a

desired haven for Lautaro in the middle of all that is

going on.

Lautaro plopped down in his seat right next

to Kearu who this time was comfortably seated

across from his longtime bandmates.

"Is everything alright," Kearu asked

Lautaro.

"Unfortunately, no," said Lautaro quietly while sniffing.

Emerson then arrived to accompany the boys, as the express train had started to continue on its path on the railroad track. She stood leaning against the compartment's doorway because she felt they were occupied. Sicur, Diamien, and Budder sat on the one-row side of the plush seats, while Lautaro, Kearu, and Sabriel sat in the row seat across from them.

"He needs to get his plane back," Emerson explained to the group, as Lautaro was silent in tears.

"It is possible we should help him get it," Sabriel suggested as he leaned closer to the group from his seat, "I might have a plan...we can go up to the King and ask politely about it."

"Oh great that will work great," Budder sarcastically exclaimed as he lifted his arms in the air, "we merely go to the King who is responsible for our suffering!"

"Definitely, it might be lethal to do such a thing," Sicur said.

"Listen, guys, I know it sounds odd, but trust me I have been in and out the castle before without getting caught, no one knows the kingdom more than I do," Sabriel said with such high confidence that one would be sure he was telling the truth.

"Why should we do that," Emerson urged the group, "we might get brutally killed by their guards, you know they do not like peasants like us

getting near the King."

"Do not worry, I will tell you guys the plan

if and once we get there," Sabriel said assuringly,

"just, trust me, I am merely trying to help Lautaro."

Lautaro elevated his head to examine Sabriel

showing a glimmer of hope for the first time in a

while in his face as he said, "You know what? I

might be willing to try to do that."

At this point, he was desperate for a solution

to get his plane back and was willing to try

anything. "How will we get there though?" he asked

him.

"Simple," said Sabriel "You are a

distinguished foreigner, right now we are in

isolation meaning he will be kind enough to let you leave the Kingdom."

"Ah, that makes sense," said Lautaro as he started to get excited with hope," but how will I get there?"

Sabriel then turned to look up at Emerson and asked, "You do not suppose your friend here would be kind to give us a ride?

"WAIT?! WHAT?!," hollered Emerson infuriated with surprise, "Why me?!"

"Simple, I think that it is the least you can do for Lautaro and after all, you did bring him along," said Sabriel slightly smiling.

Reluctantly, but also not wanting to be deemed as selfish in front of her faithful friends,

Emerson gives in to his pleas and agrees to take him

to the central kingdom to go see the king.

"Alright, I will do it," declared Emerson as she

slumped down to take a seat next to Budder,

"anyways do you guys want me to take you all

home now? It is pretty late.

"Most definitely," Budder told her, "I really

need some sleep now."

Lautaro sat down to sit next to Kearu who

had been listening to their entire conversation. He

was asked by him, "Do you mind if I come with

you?"

Lautaro looked at Kearu, surprised by the

fundamental question he had just asked him.

Lautaro then replied by saying, "Huh? If I heard you right then yes, you may come along, but what instills you to do so?"

"Oh you would be delightfully surprised," said Kearu simply as he promptly turned to look at his bandmates and ask them "Are you guys coming along?"

Diamien and Sicur looked at each other, both surprised to be allegedly asked such a burning question by their close band peer. "Uh sorry Kee, but not this time," said Diamien, as Sicur nodded his head in agreement.

"Oh well, that is totally fine," Kearu replied to them calmly.

The train then came to a halt. Emerson and Budder got up from their seats, she looked at Lautaro "Do you want to come along? We are dropping off Budder."

"Uh sure, YES," exclaimed Lautaro, having gained confidence now that there was a chance for him to recuperate his plane back. He got up from his seat to join them. They walked down the train's lane to the locomotive and got off the train after Emerson had opened its door. They walked calmly down the grassy slope to Budder's cabin. It was near the railroad track, so there was no need for them to carry a lantern as the train's lights illuminated enough through the window to the nearby region.

"Stay safe," Budder told Emerson with tears in his face as he hugged her. "Do not worry, I will be," Emerson assured him.

Budder then turned his attention to Lautaro and told him, "I may not know you well but let me tell you if you are with Emerson you will be safe. It is not about where the train is going but taking a risk and getting on aboard for a chance." He hugged him as well.

Lautaro already started feeling like part of belonging to this world, something he had never truly felt before. Budder then started heading towards his cabin, opening its front door to get in and before he closed it, he turned around one last time to smile and wave goodbye to Emerson and Lautaro. Once he got inside of his cabin, Lautaro and Emerson walked back to the train. They both got on board of the train, and Emerson went straight to start the locomotive as Lautaro went to the compartment where The Shapes and Sabriel were. Sabriel was taking a nap, so Lautaro decided to sit next to Kearu instead.

"Hey," Kearu told Lautaro, noting his arrival.

"Oh hey," Lautaro replied back before asking, "how are you?"

"Tired," inclined Kearu," however as determined as one could ever be."

Emerson then arrived to join, she sat in the seat next to Sabriel who let out a snore.

"I have to go home soon, Lautaro you can stay at my place with me and my family for the night if you would like," Emerson said, "I will drop off The Shapes and Sabriel at the town's train station."

"Sounds fine and dandy to me," said Lautaro as he let out a yawn before asking her, "What time is it?"

Emerson then looked at her clock and said it is pretty late, "It is Angelou time!"

Lautaro then began to chuckle, "wait what, do you guys not have numbers in this world?"

"Oh we do," Emerson said.

"Then what time is it," Lautaro asked her.

Not sure by what Lautaro meant, Emerson simply told him that she already told him what time it is, "It is Angelou time," she stated.

Lautaro gave her a confused look, "Huh, do you guys not use numbers to represent time?"

Emerson, highly confused by what he was saying, gave him an unsure, "No."

"Okay, that is strange," Lautaro said as he decided not to further talk on the topic anymore.

Lautaro turned to look at Kearu, and remembered the spectacle that he had put up while playing at the concert, and truly wondered what Emerson meant when he mentioned that he is a star soul. He could not help himself but ask him what a star soul is?

"Hey Kearu, are you a star soul, and what is that," Lautaro asked him.

"Ah, so you have heard," Kearu told him, "well let me say we are a unique type of people, with sky given gifts such as high levels of creativity and clair-like abilities, we have a deep connection with the stars."

"Are there more people like you out there," Lautaro asked him, intrigued to learn more about star souls.

"Yes, there are more like me out there," Kearu stated, "However people of my caliber are seen as a threat when we simply want peace above everything else."

"Ah," said Lautaro, "I think I now get what makes you star souls so unique."

It got quiet for a minute, before the train came to a halt, having arrived at the train station. The Shapes were the first ones to start heading out of the train.

As they exited the compartment, Diamien stated, "See you guys and stay safe."

"Bye guys," waved Sicur.

"I will meet you guys in the morning at what time," asked Kearu.

"At oxen time," Emerson responded to him.

"Alright got it, and I will see you guys until then," said Kearu and he left the compartment to start heading out, leaving Lautaro, Emerson, and Sabriel alone. Emerson got up from her seat and started to wake up Sabriel.

"Sabriel, wake up," she exclaimed.

"Huh, what," Sabriel said surprised and then asked, "are we at the train station yet?"

"Yes, we are here," Emerson told him as she went on to explain to him, "Meet us here in the morning at Oxen time."

"Sabriel gave out a loud yawn, got up from his seat, and before exiting the compartment, told her, "Got it!"

"Well time to go to my home," Emerson told Lautaro, leading him the way out of the train. She turned the train off and opened the slider door of the locomotive for her and Lautaro to hop off the train.

"Will your train still be here," Lautaro asked her.

"Yes, it will be," Emerson said as she continued to explain to him pointing at the other trains that were stationed at the train station," you see those other trains resting within their own

97

railroad tracks, well this track is reserved for my

train."

"That is neat," Lautaro told her as he

followed Emerson through the railroad tracks until

they reached a small staircase that led up to the train

station's waiting court area that led out into the

streets. The streets were lit up by tall lamp posts,

brightening the view of the streets, while the streets

themselves were made of cobbler.

Lautaro and Emerson walked on the street, it

was really late at night so no one was in sight

except for some of the people that worked in a few

of the shops that they passed by that were still open.

They kept walking on these cobbled streets, whilst

Lautaro found that the round, smooth sensation of

the cobbles on his shoe to be satisfying until they

reached a street that was surrounded by cabin houses.

"So this is my neighborhood," Emerson told Lautaro, "Street Berrydough!"

"It looks really neat," said Lautaro as he admired the clean streets along with the cabin houses which were all brown, but what differentiated all of them from one and another were their colorful roofs.

Most of these houses were one story high, but a few were two stories high. Their walls from the exterior were adorned in vines that had flowers growing from them. The houses had metal bars with spiral and wavy gates that led to the front yards of these homes, most of which were adorned to the liking of the owners in a variation of their preferred

or maintained floras.

Emerson led Lautaro to her home which had

a yellow-colored roof, a small garden of roses in the

grassy front yard, and a small white gate door that

led as an entrance to it. Once they had entered

through it and arrived at the front door of her home,

she knocked on it several times. Lautaro looked at

Emerson as she kept knocking on the door a few

more times, "Do not worry, they will answer

eventually, they are probably sleeping," she assured

him.

The door to her front home then opened and

a slightly chubby man came out wearing blue polka

dot pajamas.

"Eeeeey there is my daughter," he yelled out as he went to hug Emerson, revealing to be her father. Behind the plumpy man, closely followed a tall slim woman with flowy brownish-red hair and three young children. Lautaro assumed that they must be Emerson's mother and her three siblings.

After she had finished hugging her father, Emerson turned her attention towards Lautaro.

"Everyone I want you to meet my new friend, Lautaro," she told her family as she signaled one of her hands towards him.

"Hello nice to meet you all," said Lautaro while waving his hand at them timidly.

"Lautaro, meet my family," Emerson went on to say pointing at each of her family members one by one at a time, "This is my dad, my mom, and my three little siblings, Carod, Dey, and Jus!"

"Ah, well it is nice getting to know you all," said Lautaro as he started to become accustomed to being around the family.

Emerson's father had been giving Lautaro a stern look for a while before turning to Emerson to ask her," Emerson, is this your new boyfriend?"

Emerson looked at Lautaro as she turned red with embarrassment then she looked back at her dad to explain the situation to him, "No, he is not my boyfriend, he is just a friend, I will explain the rest once we are inside, he is going to stay the night with us."

Her father looked at her skeptically and then at Lautaro before walking back into the house, along with his wife and children.

"Hey Lautaro, come along," Emerson told him as she followed her family, entering her home. He followed up after her, entering their house, Emerson staying on the side of the entrance, until everyone got in, to close the door shut behind them.

Despite the house being one-story in size, it had a comfortable vibe to it, due to the warm colors of maroons, and yellows that dominated the curtains, furniture, and decor of the home. With light lamps that only further highlighted the tones of these colors as they illuminated the home in yellow light.

As he entered the living room, he was met with Emerson's mother who told him, "I will get the couch ready for you," she put over some pillows and blankets over the couch, "you must be really tired after a long day, huh?"

"I sure am Misses...," Lautaro left off his sentence indicating for her to finish it.

"Oh you can call me Misses Canope, that is the family's name," she explained as she finished setting up the couch for him to sleep in, "the bathroom is the first room to the left of the hallway lane in case you need to use it."

She then left the living room, heading into the hallway lane, seemingly entering the bedroom where she and Mr. Canope slept.

Just then Emerson arrived at the living room

from the kitchen and came to see Lautaro tell him,

"if you are hungry, my mom has made some

sandwiches, they are in the fridge, help yourself."

She then headed to her parents' room to

discuss her situation and how she planned on going

on a journey on her train with Lautaro and her

friends in hopes of getting his plane back, leaving

Lautaro alone in the living room which was dimly

lit by just one of the lamps being turned on.

Lautaro, realizing that he had not eaten a full

meal since before he left the island of Bonaire, went

to grab a grub. He walked into the kitchen, turning

the light switch on, as the room was illuminated by

a mild spherical chandelier, that was simple in

design, but still neat.

And as he went over to the table where some ham and lettuce sandwiches were laid, wrapped in a napkin, he reached out for one of them and began to eat it. He looked around the kitchen and saw a tray of cups, he grabbed one to serve himself some water from the sink's faucet that was shaped like a blooming blue flower. With a sandwich in one hand and a cup of water in the other, he sat down on one of the wooden chairs of the wooden kitchen table to start enjoying this simple meal which he was so grateful for after a chaotic venture.

While he was eating his sandwich, he could hear Emerson talking with her father some rooms down about how their journey starting the next morning is supposed to go. By the sound of their voices, he could tell that her parents were displeased about what they were hearing, but had trust in their daughter to do the correct thing.

As Lautaro finished his meal, he got up from where he was seated and began to exit the kitchen, making sure to turn the light switch off behind him. He then headed to the bathroom to utilize his basic hygienic needs, especially since after being caught up in a storm, he had been soaked and ingrained with dirt.

After Lautaro had been done utilizing the bathroom, he then headed back into the living room and went to lay on the couch that had been prepared just for him to sleep on. His head hit the especially soft pillows, a comfort which he enjoyed in this unusual land. Only wonders of thoughts were left in

his mind as to what would occur in the morning as
he slowly fell asleep.

Chapter 5:The Journey Begins

Lautaro was woken up in the pleasant
morning, by Emerson yelling at him, "Wake up
Lautaro, it is morning, it is almost Oxen time!"
He groaned as he carefully opened his eyes,
greeted by the almost blinding morning light of the
sun peering through the windows, he felt that he had
not slept enough for him to feel fully motivated to
wake up within his own merit.

He also discovered it to be annoying that
time in this world was not symbolized by
considerable numbers, especially when his beauty
sleep was interrupted by such a concept.

"Hold on, I am getting up," he grumbled as he slowly sat up on the couch and extended his arms into the air as he yawned loudly.

"So what is the plan," he asked Emerson.

Emerson, who wore off-white pajamas that had green star prints on them excitedly claimed to him, "there are grains and milk if you want some breakfast! I will be back in some minutes!"

Despite Lautaro not feeling any hunger in this particular morning, as his profound senses were adapting to the otherworldliness of where he woke up, he ultimately decided to consume something as he knew it would be a healthy option for him to do so. He got dressed and walked leisurely down the hallway to operate the bathroom, before heading out into the gourmet kitchen to promptly go eat some breakfast. Emerson soon arrived at the kitchen dressed in an outfit that seemed like a unique mixture of late 1800's fashion and a train conductor. Her brunette hair flowing waveringly in motion as she walked to the kitchen table to join Lautaro who was seated down eating some grains and milk that Emerson had put beforehand on the table for him to faithfully serve himself.

"So are you excited," she asked him as she watched him eat his grains in serenity.

"Seeing as how we are risking our lives, umm no, not really," said Lautaro, as he hurried to finish his grains.

Emerson rolled her eyes as she then told him, "Oh come on that is the thrill of it, the danger!" She shrugged.

"I guess if that is what suits you," said

Lautaro unassumingly as he got up from his chair,

having finished his breakfast, "let us go now."

"Alright," said Emerson as she got up from

her seat," However, let me go get some money for

our journey."

"Why would we need the money and where

are you getting it from," Lautaro asked her.

"Well this extraordinary journey is

undoubtedly going to be long, so the money will be

a specific need," Emerson exclaimed, "And I am

getting it from my fond father's wallet, do not worry

he will be fine with it, after all, I am his daughter."

"You seem to be a bit of a daring person,"

Lautaro noted about her, "Yet your parents seem to

want the opposite for you, how do you guys get

along?"

"Well," Emerson went on to explain as she

grabbed her father's wallet from the kitchen counter

to grab some money," they know that ultimately I

am the one in charge of my life, so they let me bet

on it for myself."

"That is interesting," Lautaro replied, as he

stood near her. Once she grabbed the money, she

made sure that her collection of keys were in her

pocket as she headed out, and then proceeded to

head out as Lautaro followed closely behind her.

Once out of the house, Emerson made sure that the

front door of it was securely locked with her key, as

Lautaro waited in the front yard, admiring the

full-bloomed roses, for her to come. Once done,

Emerson came to Lautaro, and the two opened the

small gated entrance, and began to walk down the

cobbled street.

The street was more active now than it was

morning, the sun shining bright, clouds of mystic

shapes up in the air surrounded by clever blue skies.

As Lautaro and Emerson walked down the

cobbled street to the local train station, people from

the local pop shops or who were walking in the

street would greet Emerson with friendly good

mornings, some would unexpectedly ask her if

Lautaro was her boyfriend which she would just

laugh and kindly say "no" to them.

Lautaro noticed that the residents of the

town where Emerson habited in dressed in

contemporary styles that reminded him of late 1800's fashion but with a more loose, comfortable, and shortened touch to them, he found it to be both peculiar and intriguing.

When Emerson and Lautaro arrived at the train station, it was quite busy with a lot of people, some of them waiting to ride in trains, and others being conductors prepping for their travel destination or work merit of the day.

While walking through the lively crowd at the station, Emerson and Lautaro managed to invariably find Kearu and Sabriel who were both patiently waiting for them, seated on one of the benches on the sides, and while they were together, they did not appear to make many conversations with each other.

When Kearu noticed Emerson and Lautaro properly approaching, his kind eyes lit up with pleasurable excitement as he got up from his seat and ran over to give them both a hug.

"You guys are here!" he exclaimed.

Sabriel got up from his principal seat and walked over to where they were, he waited for Kearu to finish hugging his friends as he informed them, "well guess we are starting our journey now."

"Most indeed we are, follow me," Emerson said as she led them through the crowd, slightly pushing people out of the way until they reached the staircase that led down to the railroad tracks where the ground was completely covered in stone.

While walking towards Emerson's train, they halted for a while as a train came passing by, they patiently waited for it to go by.

"Oh my, am I nervous about all this," Lautaro told his friends while they waited for the train in front of them to finish steering by. Once it had gone by, they continued walking over the rocky ground where the railroad tracks were along with the stationed trains.

When they arrived at Emerson's train, she began opening its' slider door open after unbarring it with the wood sled covering it, and unlocking the lock guarding it with her keys. She gently opened the door leading to the locomotive and stepped in as Lautaro, Sabriel and Kearu followed after her.

"You guys can go take seats at the compartment while I set the locomotive on," Emerson stated, while she rapidly closed its door behind her.

"Alright," replied Kearu, "Come on guys let us promptly go sit."

Kearu opened the spiral doorknob that led into the next section of the train where all the compartments were, he led Lautaro and Sabriel into the nearest one by as he and Lautaro took their seat in on one side, while Sabriel sat in the opposite side.

"Well, how are we feeling," Kearu asked them both after taking a deep breath.

"Nervous," replied Lautaro.

Sabriel was momentarily quiet, looking both at Kearu and Lautaro before saying, "somewhat anxious."

The express train's engine let out a terrific roar, and then the train proceeded to venture on the direct path of the railroad track that it was on. Some minutes later, Emerson arrived at the compartment in which Lautaro, Kearu, and Sabriel were. She sat down next to Sabriel, as she carefully laid out a regional map of the mighty kingdom of Alnidor in front of them on the table.

"Over here are the plan guys, we are going to be passing by the forested area, head up to the Rocky Mountains, and then, at last, arrive at the central Kingdom," she explained to them, pinpointing and gliding with her finger the locations across the map.

"It appears to be easier than I thought it would be," said Lautaro.

"Well yes, if we do not discover any critical problems," Emerson said as she started wrapping up the map.

"The comprehensive plan should be easy," said Sabriel, "but the checkpoints where there are typically going to be armed knights might pose a bit of considerable difficulty for us."

"Yes, but there is only one checkpoint we might come across within our journey," Emerson explained, "however we just have to act cool, and

they should let us continue onto our path."

"All of this sounds good to me," chimed in

Kearu to tell them, "I am positive we will make it

through!"

"Now that it appears we are all set for what

is to come, I will be over at the locomotive, making

sure we are safe on the right track," Emerson then

went on to say, "if any of you need me, come

around."

She got up from her seat, with the map

rolled up in her hand, and went to manage the

locomotive as she exited the compartment. Lautaro

was left alone with Sabriel and Kearu, and it went

silent. An awkward silence. He decided to start up a

conversation with them to formally introduce

himself as he still felt relatively new to these gentlemen.

"Um hello, everyone, I am Lautaro," he introduced himself, "I do not think that we have formally been introduced to each other or gotten to know each other well."

"Well hello there Lautaro," said Kearu with a smile, "I am Kearu, a musician, who is also leading a revolution, I am a star soul so not only do I have high intuition but also some magical abilities...and what about you Lautaro, what are your ambitions?"

"Uh me," Lautaro said as he thought out for a moment to articulate his response, "I like to write poetry, daydream a lot, as well as to travel the world and see wondrous landscapes, I especially like to get around by air on my private plane."

"Woah, that is awesome," Kearu complimented him before asking him, "So basically you fly around like a free bird, going anywhere you go, is that why you want to get your plane back so badly?"

Feeling flattered by Kearu's intrigued, appreciative question towards his love for flying by plane, Lautaro replied to him, "Oh I wish we were all truly free, and without limits, but flying by plane is the closest I will ever get to that sensation especially after years of not having any of it!"

"We are more alike than you think," Kearu told him, feeling a connection to Lautaro's thought of reason while giving him a smile that Lautaro returned.

Kearu then turned his attention to Sabriel who had been listening to his and Lautaro's conversation without saying a word, and asked him, "What about you Sabriel? Tell us a bit about yourself."

Without showing hardly any emotional range, Sabriel simply stated, "I am Sabriel, and I have been all over Alnidor and the world so I know how to get around on my own."

"Ah well that is special, being able to navigate on your own, an important skill I must add," Kearu told him.

"I guess so...," replied Sabriel and it became

momentarily quiet again in the compartment before

he spoke up again and asked Kearu, "Hey Kearu,

could you show me some of your powers."

"Well, I mostly only use them for

self-defense...or spectacles," Kearu replied, "but I

guess I can show you guys a representative sample."

Kearu then proceeded to lay out his left hand

on the table, and a small, yellow orb slowly

appeared as it illuminated its build-up.

Lautaro gasped in fascination, as Sabriel

watched in silence, appreciating the demonstration

"That is charming," shouted Lautaro in

admiration, "how is there not more people like you

out there ?!"

"There is always a possibility for there to be more star souls, some are made and some are born," Kearu went on to explain "however we are often prosecuted or slandered as our kind has the transparency in everything we do."

"Oh," said Lautaro silently noting Kearu's vulnerability is his statement, "well I wish you safety and hope everything goes right in your life."

"Yes, but star souls are said to have a direct connection to the stars," Sabriel chimed in to say, "that would make them a bit different to most of us, I would think."

"In a way yes, however, we are made of star particles, therefore it is within everybody's possibility to activate that potential," replied Kearu.

"I suppose so," said Sabriel as he slightly lowered his head to look at the ground.

It got quiet again, Kearu turned to look at the window, realizing that they would soon be passing by an interconnected bridge over a body of water between two landmasses. He immediately turned to Lautaro and asked him, "You are not afraid of heights, are you?"

"Umm not really," said Lautaro, "I spend most of my time up in the air."

"Well come on over take a look out the window," said Kearu showing Lautaro his usual, dorky smile.

Lautaro traded sitting spots with Kearu as he began to open the window, he peered out of the window and saw a splendid, beautiful scene as he looked down to a sparkly, flourishing streaming

river. He started to take a breath of the air as the

train that they were on was on the railroad track

bridge and put out his hands as he shouted out an

energetic "Woah!" out of excitement.

As the train on the track begins to head into

the landmass again, he entirely got back in the train,

closing the window behind him.

Once he was seated again in his seat,

Lautaro looked at the other two who were with him,

Sabriel gave him a nod of acknowledgment as

Kearu smiled at him and said: "One must appreciate

the beauties of life wherever one goes!"

"Truly, that is true," yelled out Lautaro.

The train then came to a sudden halt,

Lautaro assumed that they must have arrived at the

checkpoint. His assumptions were confirmed to be true when Emerson came into the compartment to inform him and his two other friends about the current situation.

"We are going to be questioned, everyone just act cool, and I will also buy some food and supplies for us as well," she told them, "now get up and follow behind me."

She exited the compartment, while Lautaro, Kearu, and Sabriel all got up to naturally follow behind her. As they followed her to the locomotive, to get off the train and Emerson was getting ready to lock it behind her, a knight in silver armor approached them and informed them, but specifically to Emerson, "I am to properly inspect the train, while you guys are out, please leave it

open."

Emerson looked at him skeptical but did not

state anything as she quickly unlocked the train

again, allowing for the knight to enter the train.

"Ok," said Emerson as she shrugged and led

her friends to the interrogative checkpoint, "well let

us continue guys."

She, Lautaro, Kearu, and Sabriel all walked

on the dirt ground, off the side of the railroad track

until they reached a staircase that led up to the

walking concrete floor that led to the small town of

Rydon. A booth guarded by four knightmen awaited

them there.

Emerson was to be interrogated if she

wanted entry into the town to buy some necessities

and food. She walked up to the booth, while

Lautaro, Kearu, and Sabriel sat down in the benches

as they were all in common to wait for her arrival in

the courting area.

"Got anything of any significance with

yourself, in the train, or with your friends," the

knight asked her.

"No, not at all sir," Emerson said, "just me

and my friends on a railroad trip."

"Alright then," said the knight as he pushed

a button in the booth that made a wooden barrier

open up, allowing for Emerson to enter the town, as

she stepped foot into it.

While Lautaro, Kearu, and Sabriel waited in

the courting area, some of the knights' men who

were guarding the courting area led their attention

towards the boys who were just silently sitting,

minding their own business.

Lautaro noticed this and asked, "why are

they looking at us?"

"Typical behavior of theirs, they will have a

problem with whoever they want to," replied Kearu.

And sure enough, the four knights instantly

begin to start walking towards them.

One of the errant knights asked Sabriel, "are

these your friends?"

"They sure are," Sabriel replied.

The same knight then went up to Kearu,

who started to get noticeably nervous and asked

him, "you guys are not hiding anything are you?!"

Kearu meekly replied, "no, not at all."

This knight then turned his attention to

Lautaro as the other three knights then began to

circle in around the boys, and noticed that his

dressing style was different and unusual.

"Just to make sure you are from Alnidor,"

the knight asked him.

"Umm, yes, very much," exclaimed Lautaro,

"I love rum pops so much!"

Sabriel could not help but to shake his head

in embarrassment as he witnessed Lautaro

awkwardly try to give a good impression as though

he pertained to Alnidor.

"Pull out the sparkle detector," the knight

commanded his fellow knights men.

Suddenly one of the knights pulled out a

small bag, he opened it up, reached in with his hand

and pulled out sparkle dust which he threw at

Lautaro who began to cough as he breathed some of it in.

The sparkle dust which was initially colorless, but sparkly began to turn red around Lautaro, indicating that he was not from Alnidor.

"Just as I thought," said the main knight who had interrogated him and his friends, "I am afraid you will be taken into custody."

All four knights started to close in on Lautaro when Sabriel got up from his seat and interrupted, "If you are going to take him, then you might as well take me too."

He then quickly stepped in front of Lautaro, shielding him from the knights.

"I do not think that this would be a good idea," he told them.

Just then Emerson was arriving at the scene

with her hands full of brown bags filled with

essential hygienic needs, food, and blankets.

"Do not aid your friends ma'am," the knight

at the booth advised her as he allowed her entry,"

they are potential troublemakers."

Standing frozen in both fear and doubt,

Emerson knew that something terrible would ensue

as she witnessed the knights men surrounding her

friends start pulling out their swords.

She gave Kearu, who was seated next to

Lautaro gripping his hand, an anxious glance,

hoping he could come up with something quick

with his star soul powers.

The knight that had inspected the train had only just arrived and pulled out his sword levelling it at Emerson.

"She does not have a necessary permit to be conducting the train," he shouted out at his fellow knights from where he was standing.

"You get rid of her, and we will get rid of her friends," one of the knights that were improperly handling Lautaro, Sabriel and Kearu said.

As the knights started to raise their swords getting ready to hack them down onto them, Kearu immediately went into action, activating his star soul powers. His eyes turned blank as red light orbs began appearing behind, he could control them at his own will with his mind. He sent several orbs towards each of the knights that were in the courting, including the one menacing Emerson and the one at the booth. These orbs turned into small explosive sparks that dazed the knights or pinched them in the targeted areas, making them back off from him and his friends immediately.

Kearu then got up from his seat, he firmly held onto and pulled Lautaro by the hand and told him, "We need to go back to the train, now!"

Sabriel followed close behind them as they started running towards the train. Emerson was already heading down towards the staircase.

As the group was running on the dirt path off of the side of the railroad track to head towards the locomotive, one of the knights jumped in front of them from the court ridge, obstructing their path.

"Not so easy," he informed them, holding out his

sword, leveling it towards them.

"Everyone behind me," Kearu advised his friends as

he stepped forward to confront the knight himself.

"What causes you to think you are doing the

right thing," Kearu inquired.

"My undisputed king gives out the orders;

he is a nobleman," replied the knight as he swirled

his sword to prove off his skills in utilizing the

lethal weapon.

"You have a lot to discover," Kearu said.

"Not as much as you do," replied the knight

as he started running towards Kearu getting ready to

nick him with his sword at any given moment.

Just as he was nearing Kearu, Kearu set his left hand out in front of him, and an extremely bright light ray of light came out, temporarily blinding the knight.

The knight fell into the floor by the unexpected attack, and he started kicking and wielding his sword in all directions, being unable to see where he was ostensibly aiming he shouted, "I will get you someday, I promise I will!"

Kearu and his friends carefully walked around the errant knight who was furiously striking the foul air on the ground as Kearu told him, "Well, I merely hope that dreary day never arrives.

"Lautaro, Emerson, Kearu, and Sabriel then hurried to get to the train's locomotive, as Emerson opened the door for her mutual friends to get in, the other knights peered over the concrete court ledge

to see their fellow knight man in a despairing state

on the ground, and thus decided not to further go

after Lautaro and his friends.

Once they had gotten on the express train,

Emerson shut the door behind them, and as she

started the locomotive after she had put her

shopping bags down she turned to look at Kearu to

tell him, "Thank you, you endure being a wonderful

man."

Chapter 6:Refuge

The train was continuing railing on its way

onward towards the King's castle as Emerson turned

its engine on.

Lautaro, Kearu, and Sabriel all headed

towards the compartment, and slumped down in

their seats, exhausted by the chaotic ordeal that they

had been met with at the checkpoint.

"Wow, that was a close one," stated Lautaro.

The express train was continuing railing on

its way onward towards the King's castle as

Emerson promptly turned its efficient engine on.

Lautaro, Kearu, and Sabriel all headed

towards the compartment, and slumped down in

their seats, exhausted by the chaotic ordeal that they

had encountered at the checkpoint. "Wow, that was

a close one," stated Lautaro.

"You can say that again," Kearu told him.

After setting the train on auto-conduct mode, Emerson walked to the compartment where her friends were, carefully carrying her shopping bags. She showed up on the compartment's doorway and with a large, beaming grin asked her friends if they were hungry.

"Definitely," said Sabriel.

"Why, YES I AM," exclaimed Lautaro excitedly.

They all then turned to look at Kearu who said, "What?" before saying "Of course, count me in!"

"Alright, perfect enough," said Emerson as she continued to mention, "but you guys are helping me, do you guys want to make mushroom pita or pasta with deer meat?"

"PASTA," yelled out Lautaro.

"I agree with you, my friend," exclaimed Kearu.

"I'm right there with you guys," Sabriel told them.

"Then what are we waiting for," Emerson asked them, "Let us get cooking!"

She then started walking down the train's lane, as her friends got up from their seats, and followed behind her as she set her bags down momentarily on the ground to begin to open the spiral doorknob that led into the next section of the train.

Once she had opened the door, she grabbed her bags from the floor and entered the room, she turned the light switch on, as she turned behind to tell her friends "Come along inside lads!" She went inside first, followed by Kearu and the Lautaro, and lastly Sabriel who stepped into the second section of the train.

Lautaro was magnified by what he saw in the second section of the train, it was a kitchen on a train! The walls of this section of the train were adorned in a painted wallpaper design of wavy flora with green and yellow-colored striped backdrop. Emerson laid her shopping bags on the counter, as she started pulling out food items from them, some

143

being vital ingredients for the pasta they were about to make, while she put the others in the cupboards as they would be for another occasion. The remaining bags that had blankets and basic hygienic utilities in them like toothpaste, toothbrushes, and toilet paper she put to the side so they would not interfere with the group's cooking area.

Emerson handed Sabriel and Lautaro some tomatoes and asked them, "do you guys know how to use knives?"

"We are talking about cooking, right," Sabriel asked her.

"Naturally I am," Emerson stated back at him as she opened up one of the slider cabinets and pulled out two ceramic knives, one for Lautaro and the other for Sabriel. "Here you go," she told them as she then ordered them to start carefully cutting

the organic tomatoes into excellent pieces.

Emerson then turned her considerable

attention to Kearu and gave him a packet of noodles

and asked him, "can you get them wet?"

Kearu then replied to her, "of course,

spaghetti is straight until it is not!"

He then rushed to the sink, grabbed a pan,

and put the noodles in it as he turned the faucet on,

making sure the water covered the noodles entirely

in the pan before setting them on the stove to let

them heat up, naturally turning the noodles to

slowly become malleable.

Emerson, on the other hand, grabbed a

ceramic knife for herself and grabbed the packet of

deer meat that she had bought from a market while

in the small town of Rydon. She opened it up, placed the meat on a cutting board of the kitchen countertop, and began to cut the meat into small bits and pieces. Once she finished that, she placed the meat into a pan, and began to cook it after she had to add salt, pepper, and other seasonings to it, separately from the noodles.

"We are done cutting the tomatoes into small bits," Lautaro announced to Emerson.

Emerson looked at the tomato bits that Lautaro and Sabriel had cut into small pieces, "well done," she told them as she grabbed another pan and put the tomatoes in them, filled it with some water before adding some herbs to it, she set it on the stove and gave a squasher to Lautaro.

"Here you go, squash the tomatoes using this until they have become purée," she told him as she handed him the metallic squasher.

Kearu had just finished emptying the water from the noodles, and as Lautaro was finishing the made tomato purée, he poured the noodles into the same pan.

"Well, it looks we are getting near a finish," Emerson stated as she checked in on the pan with the dear meat to make sure that it was properly cooked before pouring it into the same pan along with the now covered in tomato purée noodles, she grabbed a large wooden spoon from a cupboard and begin to mix all of the food around in the pan, making sure that the tomato purée was evenly spread throughout the food.

At that moment, Lautaro had an urge that he had been holding onto for a while to use a bathroom, so he asked Emerson if there were any bathrooms on the train.

"Oh," she replied to him, "the bathroom is in the next section of the train, it has everything that one would need!"

"Thank you and I will go take a look," Lautaro told her as he started walking over to the door that led into the third section of the train. He rotated the spiral doorknob to open it, and the door began to open, he peered his head in first, it was dark. Just as he was about to enter the bathroom, Emerson called his name from behind him.

"Lautaro wait," she called to him, running after him, as she had a bag with bathroom necessities in her hands.

"Here, could you put these in the bathroom, we will need them," she told him as she handed him the bags.

Lautaro took a peek inside of the bags as he grabbed onto it, there were toothbrushes, tubes of toothpaste, soaps, shampoos, and toilet papers in them.

"Wow, sincerely thank you," he said to Emerson as he looked back up to her.

"No problem, now go on," Emerson told him as she went back to the glowing stove to make sure that the homemade pasta with deer meat was ready.

Lautaro then turned around to walk into the third section of the train. He flung one of his hands around over the wall to his side, searching for a light switch. Once he found it, he turned the lights on and was surprised by what he saw in front and all around him; a bathroom that included a bathtub, two toilets within enclosed areas, and a shower stall with flowered curtains for assured privacy. The room was that of a baby blue color with painted rubber duckies as wallpaper.

He headed to one of the toilet stalls, and did his business and then washed his hands with bubbly pink soap in the bathroom's sink after unraveling the items that were in the bag and placing them in their respective spots. Instead of heading back to help his friends finish making a dinner meal, curiosity got the better of him as to what was in the next section of the train.

He started walking towards the metallic, shiny door at the end of the room that led into the next section of the train. He opened the door, rotating the spiral doorknob, and stepped into the darkness of the room. He searched for a light switch with his hands on the walls until he found and proceeded to turn it on. His view was welcomed by a homely room full of cozy beds that were connected to the walls of the room, which were adorned of an orange color tint that had paintings of orange trees on them. The only thing separating the drawings of the orange fruit from the orange backdrop being their outlines.

The room felt fruitfully toasty, as he sat on one of the beds it was beyond soft and had a small caged barrier surrounding it to make sure that one would not fall to the ground while the train was in motion. He laid out on the bed, it was gently balm and gave him a sense of peace within the midst of the greater hectic situation in which he was currently entrapped in.

As he laid there in the bed, he started wondering, going deep into his pensive thoughts about how perilous everything seemed at the moment. He felt an impulse of sadness almost where he started questioning if his life was worth continuing at this point and if there was any point in venturing out into this journey as there appeared to be no clear end goal of what he would do if he were to get his plane back especially since it appeared he

was now in another world.

Small tears started to gently roll from

his eyes, he knew he had to be strong yet the

entire situation seemed to have a tad of

impending doom to it as he knew he had

very little power in such a strange world.

The profound notions that were

overwhelmingly calming to him in all of their

apparent hopelessness were abruptly interrupted by

Emerson who walked into the section of the train

that he was in and yelled excitedly, "DINNER IS

READY!"

"Th- that is awesome," replied Lautaro with

a slight shake in his voice as he got up to take a seat

in bed.

Emerson noticed something was off with

Lautaro based on his current pose, she walked over

to the bed where he was sitting at and sat down next

to him and asked him if everything was fine. "Not

really," he replied to her, merely keeping it real, "It

is as if I have no power over anything and that in

itself makes me feel useless."

Emerson merely nodded her head while

listening to him, noting what he had said, and got

thoughtful for a minute before informing him, "We

are in an extremely difficult situation right now, but remember as long as there is any sort of love and unity among us then that is what will count in the end, in the meantime we must not show any fear when facing adversity!"

She then proceeded to hug Lautaro, who then started to break out crying, as he felt at ease to demonstrate his social vulnerability to her, but quickly wiped off his tears and started relaxing as it was unusual for him to show such emotional range.

"Come on now, the prepared food will get cold," said Emerson as she got up from the prepared bed and started to walk towards the considerable section's door to head out. Lautaro remained seated down in his bed momentarily, properly processing all of his philosophical thoughts until he felt

conclusive of them.

He then got up from his seat and promptly

ran down the train's walking lane to catch up to her.

They walked back to the train's initial section,

where the train's seats and compartments were.

Sabriel and Kearu were already there, consuming

their food and seemingly appearing to genuinely

enjoy it. Emerson and Lautaro entered the

compartment in which they were. The plates full of

deer meat spaghetti were ready on the table along

with eating utensils and napkins as they took their

respective seats to eat the food.

Once Lautaro was seated, he grabbed a wooden fork

that was set upon his plate and instantly began to eat

it. While contentedly munching on the spaghetti, he found it to be exceptionally delicious! The tomato sauce that they had made was puree-like, and the dear meat bits added a chewy, flavorful delight to the pasta. He got thirsty, so he reached out with one of his hands towards the cup that was near his plate. As he held the cup in his hand, he looked into it and saw a sparkly liquid in it.

"What is this," he asked Emerson as he turned to look at her, who was sitting beside him.

Emerson looked back at him and replied, "It is space tea, enjoy it!" She then continued to dig into her plate with her fork to obtain a mouthful of spaghetti from it. Lautaro looked at both Sabriel and

Kearu who were sitting across from him and

Emerson, they both were too busy to notice him

looking towards them as they were halfway done

eating their spaghetti. He then proceeded to take a

sip from his cup of the tea, it tasted wonderfully

weird, like a combination of watermelon, pineapple,

and orange with a hint of mint for him. He started to

wonder what it was made of if it was made of the

ingredients he assumed it was made of or if it was

made out of something else entirely.

Sabriel finished his plate first as he let out a

burp," sorry," he said.

Then Kearu finished eating his plate, to

which he offered to wait for Emerson and Lautaro

to finish their plates of food so that he can take all

the plates himself to the kitchen to wash them

himself.

"Thank you, you sure are kind," Emerson

told him as she finished her plate, handing it over to

him.

Now, Lautaro, being the only one left that

has yet to finish eating their plate of food, gave his

plate to Kearu, not having finished eating

everything completely. "Are you not hungry,"

Kearu asked him.

"Oh no worries, I am full," Lautaro told

him, lying behind the fact that he did not feel as

hungry as usual being that his thoughts of

impending doom were taking over, making him lose

his current appetite.

Kearu had a feeling that Lautaro was lying to him, but he decided not to argue with him as he knew that Lautaro was not mentally resounded for any sort of argument.

"Hmm alright if you say so," he told him, as he started stacking everyone's plates on top of each other, along with the cups and eating utensils for him to carry over to the next section of the train, the kitchen to clean up.

Lautaro looked out at the window, it was extremely dark out, nighttime had arrived as the only thing he could see was the moons' purple glow in the sky adhering to the land's trees, which they were passing by the hundreds as they all cast their figure shadows. The weariness of this view made

Lautaro yawn, he turned to look at Emerson and Sabriel and told them that he was tired.

"So am I," said Emerson as she got up from her seat, "I think I will go put the train to a stop for the night so we can rest awhile."

She got up from her seat to head towards the locomotive to turn off the engine so that the train could come to halt, leaving Lautaro and Sabriel alone in the compartment waiting for her return.

Lautaro looked over at Sabriel who started slumping in his seat, putting his arms up behind his head as he closed his eyes to rest. Lautaro felt awkward being left alone in this position with Sabriel who had an array of strangeness to him.

"Is there anything you want to say," Sabriel suddenly asked Lautaro while he was still in his resting position. It shocked Lautaro to be asked such a question out of the blue, he replied to him "Umm no, I am just tired."

"Aren't we all," Sabriel rhetorically asked him before adding on to say "life is hilarious it appears."

"Why would you say that," Lautaro asked him as he slightly leaned forward by the train's force coming to a sudden halt. "Well the fact that we both are here together," Sabriel said as he opened his eyes and sat right up ",such a rarity I would think."

Lautaro said nothing back to Sabriel as he started as he was processing what he was telling him and just as he thought of something back to say to Sabriel, Emerson who walked into the compartment where they interrupted him.

"Come on, get up guys, I will get the beds ready for you guys," she told them."Good, because I am beyond tired," Sabriel told her, getting up from his seat while stretching his arms out.

He exited the compartment, leaving Lautaro alone in it with Emerson waiting in the doorway.

"Is there something wrong," Emerson asked Lautaro as she noted his sheepish and slow attitude towards getting up. "No, nothing, I am just exhausted," he said, meeting her by the doorway of the compartment.

"All right well let us go," Emerson said as she started leading him down the train's walking lane into the next section of the train, as he walked close behind her.

She opened the door for him, as she turned the lights off of the train's major section behind them. Sabriel greeted Lautaro, who had entered the kitchen who greeted him with a "hello", he was sitting on the kitchen's countertop.

Kearu was just finishing cleaning up the last of dishes left on the sink, turned his head to look at Lautaro.

"Oh hey there, Lau," he told him, giving

him a smile and a thumbs up randomly as he started

drying up the plates he had just washed and placing

them on a tray for them to dry off.

Emerson headed towards one of the

cupboards as she eagerly grabbed the remaining

bags from them that she had obtained while she had

gone shopping during the group's stop at their

checkpoint.

She pulled out the bags, blankets and

pillows, she handed one of each to Lautaro, Sabriel,

and Kearu.

"Here you go guys," she told them. Lautaro

looked at the blanket that had been given to him, it

was soft and appeared to be made up of varying

patches sewn together to make the entirety of it. The pillow that was given to him was that of soft and plushy material enough for him to lay his head to rest, it was wrapped in a silky striped, blue bag. He thanked Emerson telling her, "I honestly do not know what I have done if I had not met you!" Kearu hugged his pillow noting, "Oh, this is wonderful."

Emerson led the boys to the third and fourth sections of the train, which Lautaro had already visited. As they entered the next section of the train, the so proclaimed "bathroom" of the train, Sabriel said in astonishment, "Wow, a literal bathroom in a train, who would have thought?"

Emerson then replied to him, "Yup, I made

sure to make this train feel like an actual home since

it is my job and where I spend most of my time on."

Kearu walked around the bathroom, getting

ahead of the group with a wondrous awe stare, he

looked all around him "This is truly isolated and

neat."

Emerson pulled and grabbed the blanket

from Lautaro's hands, before saying, "If you guys

need to use the bathroom, go ahead, I will set the

beds up for you."

"Very kind of you," Kearu said as he handed

over his blanket and pillow to her.

"Praise you," Sabriel told her as he handed

her his bed's utilities. Emerson holding onto all of

the blankets and pillows started walking into the

next section of the train. Before she closed the door

behind her she yelled to them, "I will sleep now, so

once you guys are done using the restroom then just

come on into the beds."

She closed the door behind her with one of

her hands as she firmly pressed onto the pillows and

blankets with her other hand against her chest to

hold onto them.

Once she was out of sight, Kearu began to

nonchalantly undress. Both Sabriel and Lautaro

were surprised by him doing this in front of them.

"What," Kearu said, turning to look at them,

"You guys act as if you've never seen yourselves."

"Oh nothing," Sabriel told him as he went to

use one of the bathroom stalls to do some private

business.

"It is just unusual to get undressed in front

of us with no embarrassment," Lautaro explained

his reasoning to Kearu.

Kearu shrugged his shoulders as he started

walking into the shower stall as he said, "I trust you

guys to be mature."

"Right," Lautaro said, turning to look all

around the bathroom, he did not feel the need to

take a shower as he had done so previously at

Emerson's home, and he also did not feel the need

to use the toilets so he brushed his teeth in the sink.

As he walked over there, he noticed some

toothbrushes laying out neatly in front of him of

unique colors. They each had a piece of paper

wrapped around them, taped with his and a friend's

name on there. He assumed that Emerson had

placed them there prior. Lautaro seized the blue one as that was the one with his name on it. He grabbed the toothpaste and inserted it into his toothbrush as he started washing his teeth and mouth along with it. He looked at the mirror in front of him; it was steaming up from the shower that Kearu was taking as was the entire room. He wiped the steam from the mirror and looked at his reflection. His eyes which were so usually bright with hope and optimism were now gloomy and dead. He felt saddened at the thought things would never be the same for him as he tried smiling, looking at his reflection for any remnants of himself from before as the mirror got covered up completely in shower fog. He finished rinsing and washing his teeth as Sabriel came out of a toilet stall and started washing

his hands in the sink next to the one where Lautaro
was using.

As Lautaro started heading to the latter
section of the train to fall asleep, he was interrupted
by Sabriel who had just finished washing his hands
in one of the bathroom's sinks and was wiping them
off a nearby hanging towel.

"Do you think something good will come
out of this," he asked Lautaro.

"Not sure, I would hope so, but I do not
think so," he replied to Sabriel.

Sabriel, finishing wiping his hands dry from
the towel, gave Lautaro a curious look as he started
heading towards one of the shower stalls saying
nothing. Lautaro then turned around to walk into the

next section of the train, he shut the door closed

behind him, leaving the dampness of the bathroom

and stepping into the clear coziness of the

bedrooms. There were some night lamps turned on

low volume, barely illuminating the bedroom

section of the train. Despite all the madness

expected to happen, Lautaro felt drained and at

peace in the tangy cozy dimly-lit room. Emerson

was nowhere in sight, but the beds were all neatly

made along with their blankets and pillows, so

Lautaro assumed that she had already gone to sleep

presumably in the next section of the train where

she probably had an entire room for herself. Lautaro

walked over to the same bed where he had

previously laid on when he had entered this section

of the train by himself and got in the bed. He was a

night thinker so he pondered about worldly events

from his world and how some of them are

comparable to the world in which he was in.

As he closed his eyes, he started falling

asleep, and amid the dark cloudiness of his

thoughts, he vaguely remembers hearing either

Kearu, Sabriel, or both quietly walk into this section

of the train. That was the last thing he remembered

hearing before he was completely knocked out and

went to sleep...Lautaro was suddenly woken up in

the middle of the night to the noise of something

rusting up against the train's wall from outside,

particularly from the side where he was. Creeped

out, he immediately got up from his bed. He looked

all around the bedroom of the section of the train.

They had left only one of the night lamps on, its'

illumination being set up at a tiny level. He looked

to the other beds in the room and noticed that while

Kearu laid asleep in his bed, Sabriel was missing

from his. This freaked him out into yelling out,

"Where is Sabriel?!".

This did not wake up Kearu, so he walked

over to his bed and started to gently shove him.

"Wake up, Kee," he told him. Kearu opened his

eyes and nuzzled his eyes before sitting upon his

bed. "What is the matter, Lau," he asked him "Why

are you waking me up in the middle of the night?"

"I heard a noise coming from outside, and

Sabriel is not in his bed," Lautaro explained to him.

Realizing the urgency of such a situation, Kearu's

eyes got wide open as he stared straight into

Lautaro's eyes. He got out of his bed. "No way," Kearu said as he started to glow in the dark, activating his star soul powers, to light the way in the dark path, "we have to find him."

That is when the duo heard a noise coming from ahead of the train, it was night and they were surrounded by desolate woods, so any noise within the train's distance was audible. That is when Emerson came in from the next section of the train into theirs. "What is going on," she asked them as she angrily stated, "I was woken up by all your guys' commotion."

"Lautaro here heard a noise outside and Sabriel is missing," Kearu simplified to explain to her.

Emerson gave them a confused look as she

processed what she was just told, however she

immediately knew what was going on when they all

started hearing a loud banging against the train from

one of the sections ahead of them. They all turned

to look at each other as Kearu nodded in agreement,

that they were all thinking the same thing. He told

them to follow close behind him, as he led and

lighted up the path for them. They walked over to

the next section of the train, but the sound was

coming from much more ahead of the train. They

quickly hurried into the train's main section where

the seating compartments were when the trio got

there, it became obvious that the concurring

knocking was coming from outside of the door of

the locomotive. Kearu ordered for both Lautaro and

Emerson to stay behind them, as he put one of his

hands out, getting his guard up in the case of any

surprise attacks. They slowly crept unto the

locomotive, as the knockings got louder and clearer

against its slider door.

"I'll open it," Kearu whispered as he headed

towards the locomotive's door, Emerson and

Lautaro stood by the locomotive's door that led into

the other sections of the train.

As Kearu slowly opened the locomotive's

door with one hand, he held out his other hand

ready to attack, as soon as he had opened the door

fully, someone jumped into the train immediately,

breathing heavily to catch the air. It was Sabriel!

"Close the door, close the door," he urgently remarked to his friends. Kearu, having trust in his friend, did so immediately. He slid shut the locomotive's door and quickly locked it. He then momentarily relaxed and stopped glowing, allowing for the moons' glow passing through the train's windows to light up the train. As he went up to where Emerson and Lautaro were kneeling to comfort Sabriel who was breathing heavily while sitting on the locomotive's ground.

Once Kearu had joined his friends, he asked Sabriel as to why he went outside so late at night.

Now calming down, Sabriel replied, "I woke up randomly in the middle of the night and could not go back to sleep, and therefore I decided to go for a walk in the nearby woods...the only problem is that I came across someone and they are all outside right now!"

Emerson with an even more confused look on her face asked, "Wait, Sabriel, who is outside?"

Sabriel, now relatively calm to speak in an efficient manner, turned to look at Emerson specifically and looked straight into her eyes.

"The knights," he told her before turning his head to also look at Lautaro and Kearu to say, "they are here, the king's knights are here."

Hearing this, Lautaro started to freak out at the realization of the grave situation they were in. That is when the crew of friends on board of the train started hearing sharp wedges come down hacking against the train's walls from the exterior.

"Oh no," shouted Emerson, angrily, "they are ruining my train!" She got up from kneeling and hurried to turn on the locomotive's engine.

Kearu helped both Sabriel and Lautaro get up from the ground, as he handed each of them one of his hands, he was strong enough to do so.

"Let us get buckled up in the compartments," Kearu told his two friends once they both were facing to look at him. He led them there, opening the door via the spiral doorknob to reach the next section of the train. They sat in the nearest compartment, and as Lautaro was sitting down next to the window, he was jumped by a sudden hack against the window that cracked it. It was one of the knights outside hitting the window of the compartment where they were seated. "Do not get near the window," Kearu urged him as he put his arms around Lautaro tightly and pulled him towards him.

The train then let out a loud "choo-choo", signaling that the train's engine had started, that is when the train started motioning. The knights from outside kept hacking their swords against the train's walls and windows, shattering them in the process. They would yell out to the group vile statements like, "We are going to get you eventually!"

The train started speeding away, and despite the knights knowing that they possibly could not catch up to them by foot, they now knew they tracked the route that they were taking. Once they were out of danger, Emerson joined the compartment where Lautaro and their other friends were seated.

She sat next to Sabriel, who was sitting on the opposite side of Lautaro and Kearu. "We are safe for now," she told them all, "I will be keeping an eye on the train, so you guys can just go back to your beds to sleep."

"I am a bit shaken," Lautaro said, who was still being held tightly by Kearu with one of his hands over his shoulder. It was dark in the train, as they had not turned the lights on with the exception of those in the locomotive, only thing brightening up the area being the moon's light, so they could see each other's visages in midst of the lowlight. Uncertainty and fear being clear across all their faces. That is when Emerson turned to look at her train's windows and realized that they had been shattered by the knight's swords.

"What gobblers," she stated angrily, "Will have to get that fixed soon."

She then got up from her seat and started to head out of the compartment. She turned to look at her friends one last time while standing in the compartment of her train to tell them that they can go back to their beds to sleep if they want to.

"I think we will stay here," Kearu told her, "We just escaped a dangerous situation so we will stay here for comfort reasons." Lautaro could feel Kearu's arm that was over his shoulder slightly trembling."Alright," said Emerson as she turned to leave the compartment that they were in.

"Kearu, are you nervous," Lautaro asked him."Y-yes, I am," Kearu replied to him, "This whole situation made me realize how truly vulnerable we are."

Lautaro got closer to Kearu to attempt to comfort him, "Just breathe, my friend, just breathe."

Kearu did as Lautaro told him, calming down slowly, but surely.

While calm, tears started rolling from Kearu's eyes, they were sparkly in nature, being noted under the moon's eternal glow. "I do not want to lose you guys," Kearu said in the midst of tears," like I lost my family to the violence of the kingdom."

That is when Lautaro fully embraced

Kearu's hug, now cuddling closer with him. Sabriel,

who was sitting on the opposite side from them, got

up from his seat and sat next to Kearu. It was

complete silence in the darkness, only low light

from the moons, transcending to where the boys

were seated together. Sabriel put his arm around

Kearu and got close to him. That is when Lautaro,

Kearu, and Sabriel all cuddled up together, their

presence with one another keeping each other sane,

and safe as they all processed their lives at the

moment while attempting to go to sleep. And once

they were asleep, they had wondrous dreams of a

better tomorrow despite the crude environment that

faced them all around in Alnidor.

Chapter 7:Emerson's Grandparents

Lautaro woke up, not by the sun's brilliant light, but by Kearu who gently shoved him back and forth to let him know that it was time to wake up. He opened his eyes and saw it was morning. The sunlight beamed directly through the express train's rose windows. He turned to look at Kearu, who was directly looking at him in the eyes, his brown eyes consoling him as they grounded him in reality to know where he was.

"Get dressed and go out," said Kearu, "it is quite a view."

He then got up from his seat, and before he exited the compartment to head towards the capable locomotive, he told Lautaro to make sure to meet him and their friends outside.

Leaving Lautaro alone in the compartment, he stretched his arms out to better flex his muscles, and he then peered out through the nearby window lane whose glass was now shattered, as he walked down the train's lane to head towards the bedroom section of the train where the rest of his clothes were. In the ground lay his pants and shoes, he grabbed his pants first and put them on. He then leaned on the edge of the bedframe to slip his shoes on to tie them, and while doing that his mind wondered as to what may be ahead of him for the day.

After getting dressed, he took a look through the one of the closest windows where he was standing and saw endless beautiful, green fields of grass, brightened by such beautiful scenery, his moods heightened, and he started running down the train's lane as fast as he could until he reached the locomotive. Once there, he saw that its slider door was open, so he got out of the train and stepped foot into the verdant ground, where he encountered Sabriel, Emerson, and Kearu who were all having a conversation to each other about their favorite colors and what they meant to them.

He walked up to him, and Emerson noticed him first as she ran up to hug him. "How is everything," she asked Lautaro.

"Fine, I suppose," he replied to her, "still shaken by what happened last night, but this view is so beautiful it is brightening up my moods."

"I think I will walk uphill," Sabriel said as he started walking towards a small dirt path that led to the other side of the slight slope they were on.

"Come along with us," Kearu told Lautaro as he followed behind Sabriel, "It might be of a righteous attitude."

He led Lautaro up to the hill as Emerson stayed behind to close and lock up the locomotive's door behind them before running to catch up to the guys. While walking on the dirt path trail, the view astounded Lautaro, they were on a mountainous region that was green and fertile with grass, the skies were blue, clear with a few clouds present.

The sun was beaming cheerfully. They started walking on a trail that led up to a slope.

"So your grandparents live here," Lautaro asked Emerson.

"Yes, sir, they are personal people," she said.

For the first time in a while, Lautaro felt at peace, he ensured to enjoy everything about his surroundings as he walked.

The group soon arrived at a small cabin, which is Emerson's grandparents' home. She got ahead of the group to get to the cabin first as she excitedly knocked on its front door once she got there. It took a moment or two for her grandparents to respond as they opened the door, and as soon as

they saw Emerson standing outside with a smile,
they greeted and hugged her.

"Gentlemen, these are my grandpar-," said
Emerson not finishing her sentence, as she was
interrupted by a dark dog that came, running out out
of the house, passing underneath her legs and
running up to where Lautaro, Kearu, and Sabriel
were standing, greeting them by allowing them to
pet him, despite them being strangers, yet he sensed
their good energy as they came with Emerson.

"Aww, he is so cute," Kearu said as he
kneeled to pet the dog who appeared as a dark
shadow out in the bright fields, "what is his name?"

"His name is Mist," Emerson's grandma
replied.

"Are these your friends," asked the grandpa who just noticed Emerson's friends standing not too far away from her.

"Yes, they are" replied Emerson while yawning to explain, "we are on a journey."

"Ah, I see," her grandpa told her, "I do not suppose I tire you."

"I am," said Emerson before asking him, "do you guys have any place in your cabin where I could go to sleep?"

"Oh come inside, Em, I will set up the bed for you," said her grandmother.

Emerson's grandmother then led her to the inside of the cabin, she was beyond tired from having conducted the train all night long, to keep an eye out to make sure that she and her friends would not get ambushed by the King's knights any longer

for the remainder of their trip until they had arrived

at her grandparent's. She went inside their cabin,

leaving her grandpa alone with her three friends and

Mist.

"I suppose you boys could use some

catering," said the grandpa, "come on in."

Kearu got up from the ground who had been

petting the dog.

"You sure seem to like dogs," Lautaro noted

of him.

"Yes, my family and I had several," Kearu

said with a tone of happiness as he let out his dorky

smile, which faded away immediately.

Lautaro wondered what had happened to

Kearu's family, and what was the dismay going on

in his head. As the boys followed Emerson's grandpa into the cabin along with Mist, the dog, Sabriel asked him, "Sir, how may we address you and your spouse."

By then they were all in the cabin, and as the grandpa closed the door behind them, he turned to look at Sabriel and told him, "My name is Lef, and my wife's name is Mel."

"Feel free to hang out wherever, as long as you guys do not cause havoc," said the grandpa as he started walking towards the kitchen, "just wait until Emerson gets up."

"Don't mind if I do," said Sabriel as he sprawled out on one of the couches to rest, while Kearu walked over to the only other couch in the living room to take a seat to rest while Mist

accompanied him and sat right next to him.

Lautaro walked around the living room,

inspecting the pictures and home décors on the

walls. It was of intrigue to him as he noticed

pictures of Emerson's grandparents when they were

young hanging from the walls. He saw a clock up

on the wall, he had been interested in how the

people in this strange world measured time. He kept

looking around at the pictures and decorations

dangling from the walls when he came across a

picture in black and white of a man he presumed

was Emerson's grandpa when he was young as his

facial features resembled his standing along with

another man who was wearing a coat and a young

girl with wavy light hair, they were in what

appeared to be a commercial center, perhaps amid a protest.

As he leaned closer to inspect the picture more, he heard Mel, Emerson's grandma call out to him and his friends from the kitchen's doorway, "Lef told me to tell you that the soup is ready if you boys are hungry."

Startled by the unannounced announcement, Lautaro turned around and headed into the kitchen, Kearu stayed behind to wake Sabriel to get up so he could go eat something. Kearu and Sabriel soon joined Lautaro, who was already seated down eating carrot soup from a bowl . Mel attended the kitchen, offering the boys some ginger lemon tea. Lautaro felt a sense of comfort and gratefulness at the hospitality that the grandparents of Emerson were displaying to him and his friends.

Lef sat down at the table with the boys and asked them with a stern face, "What is the journey you guys are going on, really about?"

Lautaro looked at him, "My plane, sir, we hope to get it back."

Lef asked him, "from whom?"

The boys all got quiet for a moment. "From King Hansen," said Lautaro quietly as he lowered his head slightly.

Lef looked even more upset at the mention of the King's name.

"He is a very irrational man, the kind to torture someone to death over the pettiest of things,

I would know first hand being under his rule since I was a child," said Lef sternly.

Mel, who was washing some dishes in the kitchen's small sink then chimed in to say, "I hope you youngins are aware of the dangers that this could lead to, it is a serious matter.

"With all due respect, it is a very dangerous journey," said Kearu, aiding his friend's reasoning," however Lautaro needs to get his plane back, he is not from our kingdom."

"Then where is he from," asked Lef.

Sabriel and Kearu both turned to look at Lautaro, signaling for him to explain his situation.

"I am from another world," said Lautaro who turned from giving his friends a confused look to looking at Lef with slight intimidation in his face," the world you guys inhibit from it is nothing like mine from what I have seen on maps."

Mel looked a bit surprised at this statement as she gave Lef a look of acknowledgment over what he might be thinking.

Lef took a deep breath and closed his eyes before telling all who were present in the kitchen, "I was once told by a now gone, but great man many years ago that a day would come where someone not from this earth would come to save us, perhaps it is you, however, I no longer believe in that kind of stuff, at least not how I use to when I was younger."

"Me," asked Lautaro, "Oh sir, I am sorry but I am not up to no savings, I just want to get back to my home, my world."

Lef started laughing, mocking him, "And how do you suppose to get back home if you are not from this earth? Either way, you are stuck in this world, a stateless person you are!"

Lautaro got angry by the old man's lack of faith.

"Even in my world I was stateless for most of my life, but that did not discourage me from pursuing my dreams," said Lautaro firmly as he started sitting up in the chair he was seated in," a person's national identity is just merit that we place ourselves on each other."

"Try having more faith, everyone," said Kearu, noting a growing intensity in the suite's ambiance, "Right now we do not need any divisions."

"Divisions, divisions, divisions," muttered Lef angrily, "Blind divisions cause hate, and most are to submit to them. I dislike that, but even in my rebellious, younger years that was the norm.

"Yes, but divisions are a part of human nature," Sabriel stepped in the discourse, "Without them, we have no identity."

"Correction, differences do not cause divisions, they only synergize our society to become stronger," said Kearu.

"You know something about you seems bright," said Lef turning to look at Kearu, "you remind me of a man I knew before, I have a picture with him and -er a young girl from that time in our living room if any of you came across it."

He immediately turned to look at Lautaro, "Go on with your journey, just make sure nothing happens to Em."

"I can't pro-," Lautaro's words were cut short as Emerson stepped in the kitchen and interrupted the group's discussion probe by asking them, "How is everybody doing?"

"Pretty well," said Lautaro in a monotone.

"Come on Em, take a seat, and I will prepare some carrot soup for you," said Mel hurrying to attend the meal for her granddaughter, as she grabbed a bowl she had just finished washing, dried it with her apron and poured in carrot soup from a large pot on the stove.

Lautaro had just then finished eating the last spoonful of his soup, so he got up from his seat, offering to Emerson and told the group, "I'll be in the living room."

He then walked out of the kitchen, everyone stayed silent as he exited the kitchen because they were judging his demeanor or processing the entire situation. Lautaro walked over the carpet floor and laid on the ground of the living room, and as he lay on the floor, he once again got pensive into his thoughts, reflecting on his life, wondering if this journey was even worth it. Mist, the dog who was laying on one couch got off of it and accompanied Lautaro on the floor. He did not say a word to the dog as he gently patted it, while lost in his thoughts as usual. He started feeling a sense of wariness and impending doom. He heard some footsteps coming into the living room, and when they got near him,

Lautaro looked up at their face and realized that it was Kearu.

"Oh hey Lau, doing good," Kearu asked him.

"Yes, just tired," said Lautaro softly as he closed his eyes to begin to rest.

Kearu knew that Lautaro was tired so he went to sit in on one of the couches, just resting as well, while Sabriel walked in the living room as well and sprawled all over on the other couch, seeing as how his two friends were all resting in their respective spots. The boys did not talk much to each other surprisingly, probably because they were all exhausted from the trip and its constant mishaps. They could hear Emerson discoursing the journey to her grandparents in the kitchen. Lautaro who slightly started to fall asleep as all was quiet in the

cabin and the temperatures were the perfect cool

type, could note the tone of Emerson's grandpa

scolding her for going on such a risk induced

journey, but all the sound was starting to drown out.

As Lautaro with his eyes closed to rest was

about to fall asleep, he was alarmingly awoken up

by Mist's sudden, loud barking which made him

open his eyes immediately.

"What is going on," he thought as he started

to sit up.

Someone or something was knocking

harshly on the door.Mel ran out of the kitchen and

into the living room to peer in through the peephole

"It is the King's knights," she said alarmingly,

turning to look at everyone who was in the living room.

"Oh shoot," said Lef who was walking into the living room from the kitchen to take a look through the front door's peephole, as Emerson walked close behind him, "This is only going to lead to disaster, Mel lead them to the underground tunnel, immediately."

"No, n, no," said Emerson, as she walked in front of her grandfather, realizing what he meant and told him, "you guys have to come with us!"

"Trust me, if we do that then we will all be doomed," said Lef as he hugged his granddaughter before looking her straight in the eyes and telling her, "these savages do not know when to stop, and besides me and your grandma have both lived

fulfilling lives."

Emerson started to tear up as she came to

the realization of what her grandfather meant. The

knights would stop at nothing to get in the cabin as

they had a clear suspicion that she and her friends

were hiding there, and it also means that if someone

does not stay behind to hold them up then they will

all die.

Mel walked over to where Emerson was

standing, crying, and joined Lef to hug her. Lautaro

and Kearu then went to hug their friend, and Sabriel

accompanied them as Mist attempted to do the

same, standing on his hind legs.

The group hugged Emerson, and in the midst of doing so as the group's secondary lovable silence, Kearu whispered to Emerson "Nurture can heal anyone, let us go Emerson before it is too late." The short-lived comfort for Emerson by hearing Kearu's affirming words while also being hugged by all those close to her was cut short immediately by the knight's hacking their swords against the wooden cabin's front door. The group immediately stopped hugging out of necessity to do so and start taking action.

"Take Mist with you guys," Lef told them as he started walking to his cabin's front door," he might be helpful."

"I will always love you, grandpa," Emerson told him as she prepared to leave him alone.

"I will too," her grandpa told her, keeping a

stern look on his face, trying his best told back his

tears."

"Come on, I need to get you guys out of

here," Mel commanded Emerson, grabbing her by

the shoulder to signal her to get moving.

"Goodbye grandpa, I love you a lot,"

Emerson said as an endless stream of tears of

extreme sadness and hopelessness were coming out

from her eyes, as the last thing she saw before she

left the living room was Lef preparing to open the

door.

Lautaro who had been quiet about the current

situation was extremely scared of what was

happening, he felt an extreme sorrow of sympathy

towards Emerson as he knew what it was to lose a

family member before your eyes as was what
happened to him when his father was deported
when he was only three years old. Emerson with
tears in her eyes, and her friends, along with Mist
were led by Mel to the closet of her and Lef's
bedroom where there was a small hidden door that
led to an underground tunnel. When Mel showed
them the secret door to the underground tunnel, she
gave Emerson the news that she will have to leave
them from this point onwards as she can not leave
Lef behind alone and that she wishes them the best
on their journey, as she shut the door on them
locked closed after Emerson, her friends and Mist
had crawled into it, and she hid it behind some
clothes. Emerson had become immobilized by the
knowing fact that her grandparents would most

likely end up being killed by the knights, she

remained seated on the ground. Whereas her friends

had gotten up, standing still, ready to get out of the

tunnel as soon as possible.

"Emerson, we need to go now," Kearu told

her.

Emerson remained seated on the cold stone

ground, not saying anything, just crying from the

shock of everything. Kearu then turned to look at

his fellow friends and told them to start running out.

"Lautaro, if you can, grab Mist in your arms

and take him with you," Kearu ordered him.

Lautaro looked at the dog who was in a

canine sitting position, the dog looked up at him

with its tongue out and wagging tail.

"Alright, let's see how heavy you are,"

Lautaro said as he grabbed the dog with both of his

arms and struggled to lift him up and carry him,

declaring out, "alright, got him!"

"Good," Kearu said, letting out a small

laugh, as he immediately went back to a serious

face expression to tell him and Sabriel to start

heading out.

Lautaro, carrying Mist in his arms, and

Sabriel were running ahead towards the other end of

the tunnel, as Kearu stayed behind to pick up

Emerson in his arms and carry her out.

"I am going to get you to safety," Kearu told

her.

Emerson did not say anything or reply back

as she felt the need to rest and process everything

that had just occurred. They all eventually reached

the end of the tunnel, and as they were running

through the tunnel, they realized that there were a

lot of rabbits on the ground, and as they got out of it

through what appeared a rabbit hole, they realized

that it was nighttime, the two moons, one blue and

the other pink creating a low-dim purple glow for

them. Lautaro who was carrying Mist in his arms

released him onto the ground and that is when the

group started running hysterically towards the train.

They ran down the dirt path slope to the train, the

only light source in the mountainous region where

they were being the cabin of Emerson's

grandparents which was now on fire. The knights

were out of sight, yet Lautaro felt paranoid over the

fact that they could literally appear out of nowhere

213

when he least expected it. Emerson once she saw

the flames that were slowly burning down her

grandparent's cabin, begin to ball out crying.

"Calm down, Emerson," Kearu, who was

holding her in his arms, told her, trying to calm her

down. Knowing that it would not be the right time

to ask Emerson to give them the keys to open the

train, Kearu advised Sabriel, and Lautaro to work

together to open the train. Sabriel and Lautaro

jogged to a spot near one of the train's shattered

windows. Lautaro helped Sabriel climb onto his

shoulders, so he could reach to get in the train

through the window's scope. Sabriel slithered

through the train, falling on one of the

compartment's couch-y seats.

"You good," Lautaro yelled from outside.

"Yes, I am," Sabriel replied back, "Get ready because I will be opening the locomotive's door soon.

Lautaro then walked over to where Kearu, who was holding Emerson who was now weeping in silence in a frozen stare, were all along with Mist by the locomotive's slider door.

"How are you feeling," Lautaro asked Kearu.

"Tired, but I have to be strong," he told him, turning to slightly look at him.

Lautaro admired Kearu's eyes as they were completely dark, so dark that their figures were immediately visible under the moons' low dim. Their staring into each other's eyes was broken up when they heard some commotion coming in from the locomotive, they both turned to look straight forward.

"I cannot wait to get some sleep," claimed Lautaro as he let out a yawn.

"Yeah...me too," said Kearu, as the locomotive's door slid open.

"Well, come on aboard," Sabriel told them as he stepped to the side, to give them enough space to get on the train.

Kearu gently laid Emerson over on the train's edge, as he got in it himself, she was just looking straight forward into space, with tears coming from her eyes. Knowing that Emerson was mentally not in the right place to conduct the train, Kearu carried her and rushed over all the way to the last section of the train to where her bedroom was.

Once there, he laid Emerson on her bed and told her

to rest and take her time grieving. Lautaro had

grabbed Mist in his arms and placed him aboard of

the train. Now as he was climbing himself to get on

the train, Sabriel reached out and gave him a

helping hand.

"Let me help you out here," Sabriel told

him, grabbing onto to pull him in the train. Lautaro

thanked him, turning his attention to Kearu who

walked in the locomotive.

"Hey," Lautaro told him before asking,

"Who is going to conduct the train?"

"Now that everyone was on board the train,

Sabriel closed the locomotive's door behind them,

before joining both Lautaro and Kearu, where they

were standing."

"I will conduct the train," Sabriel told them,

"you guys can help me if you want."

"Sounds good," Kearu said while adding on,

"Emerson really needs a break from this."

Lautaro asked Sabriel, "Do you have any

experience conducting trains?

"Yes, I do," Sabriel assured him before

revealing to him, "I used to steal them all the time."

Lautaro let out a random laugh by the

unexpectedness of this surprising fact that Sabriel

had just told him and Kearu about.

"Well let us get moving," Kearu told both of

his friends, "We are now close to getting to the

King's castle!"

Lautaro headed out to the following train

section, where the compartments were, he sat on

one of the train seats and started meditating in optimistic thoughts to start relaxing his mind. Kearu in the meantime aided Sabriel in figuring on how to use the train. While Mist walked up and down on the train's main lane, excitedly wagging his tail. Extremely fatigued from all the commotion, Lautaro fell asleep...

Chapter 8:Greed's Creature

The train's rocky motion awoke Lautaro suddenly.

It was silent except for the constant clamors that the train was making by coming upon bumps, rumbling constantly it was.

He got up from his seat and walked up to look down the train's lane, there was no one in sight.

Peering at the window lanes from afar, it was dark outside, so he assumed that it was still the middle of the night, so it had probably not a lot of time had passed since they had escaped the knights.

He headed towards the locomotive, where he found Sabriel managing the train, while Kearu was seated on the floor with Mist laying near him, the two just relaxing.

"Why is the train rocking so hard," Lautaro asked them.

"Go look out and you tell me," said Sabriel.

Lautaro walked back to the compartment where he had been napping and took a peek out of its window panel, and he saw that they were in the depths of a rocky valley, surrounded by large, grey-colored strong mountains. He then put his head back in the train, and walked back to the locomotive where his friends were and asked them, "It looks rough out there, where are we?"

"We are in the rock valley," Sabriel explained to him before turning to tell him and Kearu, "You guys might want to get seated tight, I have heard stories of a mighty creature appearing to people around here."

Lautaro turned to look at Kearu who gave him a small smile and nod, as he stood up, and he joined Lautaro to walk over to the following section of the train to get seated in one compartment immediately, along with Mist, who kept right behind them.

Kearu reached out to grab the dog within his arms as he buckled up tight.

While Sabriel stayed in the locomotive, running the train, he seated and buckled himself up in the conductor's seat, preparing for any turbulent challenge to come.

While the train kept rocking asways, Kearu noticed Lautaro's somber facial expression to which he tried comforting his friend by telling him

"Do not worry, past this is the castle," with another smile of encouragement. They were quiet as the train kept bumping upon rocks, making them bob around in their seats. They remained silent seated in their seats.

When they heard a large drift of rocks

shattering from afar. Lautaro stretched his neck out

of the window panel to his side and looked out.

What he saw was a mountainous rock

starting to break apart, however, a figure started

forming and emerging from it to become its own,

separate entity from the mountains, it shifted to

building the figure of a Minotaur, branching off to

move on its own from the mountainous valleys.

Lautaro put his head back in the train, as he

turned to ask Kearu, "Did you see that, what is it?!"

Kearu, replied, "It is greed's creature."

Lautaro, both frightened and tickled, turned

to look back at the creature through the window

panel.

It was an enormous Minotaur figure, made of pure rock stones, grey, mostly, however, the moon's light made it have a bit of a natural stony sparkle to it. The creatures' eyes and the cracks on its body slowly illuminated in a green glow.

It started breathing, signaling that it had come alive.

"That must be the legendary creature everyone talks about," said Kearu," it looks cool!"

"Well, what does it want," Lautaro asked him.

"I do not know," Kearu said, "I do not think it has good intentions."

Lautaro was both shocked at the sight of such an enormous creature, he had seen nothing like this before in his life!

His amusement then soon turned to horror, as the Minotaur started running towards them.

"Oh-oh, I think he is heading towards us," exclaimed Lautaro in panic as he reached out to hug his friend to attempt to remain in ease.

"Sabriel hurried the train," Kearu yelled out from the compartment, trying to keep his cool, "We are almost at the central kingdom."

Sabriel was managing the train, he started speeding the train when he saw the enormous creature running towards them.

In the meantime, the train's acceleration caused Emerson to be awoken as it sped up faster as she fell to the ground, from its rumbling. Without knowing what is going on other than that train was going on at a hectic speed, she held onto the edge of her bed with a firm grip of both of her hands as to not be shaken around the room, she felt a mix of emotions as she was trying to figure what was going on, she felt anger, sadness, and despair all at the same time!

Sabriel accelerated the train to full speed, which made Emerson feel the forces of gravity and speed pushing her towards the back of the train. She was starting to feel a bit dazzled out, but she was safe for as long as she could hold onto the edges of the bed bunk.

The Minotaur ran ahead of the train towards the tunnel entrance, and started reaching out with one of his hands and covered the entrance to the tunnel that led to the central kingdom with it, blocking the train's pathway.

"Oh great," yelled out Sabriel angrily, he gently put the train to a steady halt and went back to the compartment where Lautaro and Kearu were seated to give them the terrible news that their path had been obstructed by The Rock Minotaur.

"Realistically, there is not much we can do now," Sabriel told them, as he leaned on the doorway of the compartment to let out an exhausted sigh.

"No, no we are almost at the central kingdom," Lautaro cried out, as he was trying his best to hold up his tears, "We have to get there somehow!"

Kearu turned to look at him, "I am sorry, but unless you have rock climbing experience I am not sure that there is much we can do." He then proceeded to give Lautaro a heartwarming hug, comforting by telling him, "You can stay with me if you don't know where to go."

Just then Emerson came in storming angrily into the compartment where they were, she angrily stated, "Could any of you tell me what in the stars is going on?"

Before anyone could tell her anything about the current situation, they heard The Minotaur make a loud bellow before it said with its' mighty, roaring voice, "Come out!"

Emerson jumped, startled by fear and hurried to take a look out of her window and let out a startled scream, before going back in the compartment and declaring to her friends, "Okay, I am sorry but this is just too much, I am starting to think that this whole thing was a mistake!"

They then heard The Minotaur get closer to the train, taking its handoff from covering the central kingdom's entrance tunnel. Its' heavy footsteps made the floor tremble and it said, "Come out!"

"I think we should do as it says just to be safe," Sabriel told the group, "Try not to think the worst."

The group of friends left Mist in the train, as they all got out of the train and walked around it to the side where The Minotaur was standing, facing the train. Once out in the rock valley, The Minotaur crouched close to where the four friends were standing, it let out a humongous breath that merely

knocked them off their feet.

"What is your purpose here," The Minotaur

asked them.

"W-we are to go to the central kingdom,"

Lautaro told him, as he got up to stand.

"For what purpose," the Minotaur asked

him.

"We want to get Lautaro's plane back,"

Kearu told The Minotaur, stepping in to speak up

for his friend, Lautaro, "The king has it."

"And why would you trust the king," the

Minotaur asked them, "He is a greedy man, like

me."

"With all due respect, we understand that,"

Kearu assured him, "However it is the only way for

Lautaro to get his plane back and return to his

home."

"Is that so," The Minotaur said, turning his

attention to Lautaro, "You should know better than

wandering around to places you don't know."

Lautaro felt a droplet on his hand, he turned

to his friends who showed similar attitudes of

interest over the sensations, that they were all

feeling alike.

Kearu then looked up at the greying skies

and said, "It looks like it will rain."

The Minotaur moved his head up to look at

the sky and said, "hmmm look at the rain, how

fragile and collective it is."

His appearance turned slicker as it started

raining harder, like a rock out in the cool rain

getting wet by its prancing droplets.

"I think I better let you guys go for now,"

The Minotaur told them.

"Impressive stuff," Sabriel said.

"Before you go, may I ask what you are,"

Emerson asked him

The Minotaur got silent, the group waited

for his response as the only noise they could hear

was the downpour of the rain palpitating on the

ground.

The Minotaur responded, "I do not know

what I am for they made me from men's greed."

Lautaro then wondered if The Minotaur

worked as some checkpoint guard into the kingdom,

but he dared not ask him anything.

The Minotaur started heading out, walking

back to the mountainous rock where he had

emerged from, its large footsteps, continuing to

make the ground's floor shake.

"Thank you for letting us go," Kearu yelled

at him as he was leaving.

"Do not thank me," The Minotaur replied, as

it started to slowly submerge with its mountainous

rock.

"Those that pass shall see what is ahead,"

said the rock Minotaur in a loud voice as the last of

his visage submerged into the mountainous rocks

becoming one with them again.

"Wow, that was strange, so strange," Emerson said as she was the first to start heading back to the train, "no time to be standing out here getting wet."

As Lautaro, Kearu and Sabriel all followed Emerson back to the train, he wondered if there was any sort of significance in the words that the Minotaur had told him, the entire ordeal appeared to be an enigma of sorts that was now merely a recent memory of his. Once in the train, Sabriel offered to conduct the train for the remainder of the journey so Emerson could mentally rest and take her time processing her mind's notions.

"Thank you," she thanked him as she headed to the main compartment to take a seat. She was greeted by Mist, the dog who brought her a smile for the first time in a while. She was later joined by Kearu and Lautaro.

Once everyone was set in their seats, the train's engine turned on, letting out a loud "choo-choo" as it continued on its way towards the path towards the central kingdom. The train entered a tunnel, it was dark, but there was a light at the end of it...As the train got out of the tunnel, it entered the track that led to the central kingdom.

"We are finally here," hollered Kearu excitedly.

Chapter 9:Arrival At Last!

Coming out from a pitch-black dark tunnel and into a well-lit environment by the sky's brilliant sun, an unobstructed view of a magnificent town developed. Lautaro, at the realization that they had arrived at the kingdom, unbuckled himself. He stood up and opened the train's window, as he looked out through the window, it was sunny and bright; the kingdom was full with houses made of wood painted in every shade of pastel colors, and there were also small shops with windows that displayed wonderful pastries and fashionable jewelry along with clothes on full-display for the common folk on the streets to admire through the glass windows.

As the train continued on its path to the kingdom's train station, Lautaro was surprised to not only see other humans but humanoids as well, who were walking among the streets of the kingdom just like anyone else. Most of the humanoids were

ogre-like and trollish, however, Lautaro knew that it
would be smart not to make any assumptions about
them based on their appearances.

He also noticed that the majority of the
individuals who occupied the kingdom's streets
wore majestic robes, that swayed fabulously as their
bearers were in motion.

It was a wonder of a sight that fully
enchanted Lautaro's full attention. His attention
then turned over towards the castle of the kingdom,
that heavily loomed over the town. It was a large,
mystical castle that appeared to be made out of
pearly jewels. The sun shone on its pearly white
exterior walls, enacting its' wondrous energy to
augment over the entire kingdom in its full
prosperity.

"That is the King's castle," said Kearu, "We are going to go up there!"

"I am nervous," said Lautaro, as he sat back down in his seat after having looked out of the window panel to take a glimpse at the mystical sceneries that the kingdom had to offer.

The train shortly after came to a halt, as Sabriel walked into the main compartment to announce their concrete arrival at the kingdom.

"Well we are here," he yelled out as he wailed out his arms in the air excitedly.

"This feels like a full relief to me," said Lautaro, as he let out a satisfied sigh while simultaneously closing his eyes momentarily and let out a large grin, as he proceeded to hug Kearu tightly.

"Alright, we should all discuss the plan," said Kearu feeling flattered, as he kindly pushed Lautaro off of him "To discuss how this is going to go."

"For sure," said Lautaro as he opened his eyes, however, his huge grin remained intact, revealing a state of pure joy.

Once Sabriel had made sure that the train had been stationed properly, he went to take a seat within the same train's compartment where Mist and his friends were seated to discuss their next course of action.

"I will go to the castle first," Sabriel told them as he went on to explain their plan, "I will go under the disguise of having a message for the king, this should soften them up to accepting Lautaro's entrance."

"Will I go alone," asked Lautaro, presently showing a bit of doubt that was present in his eyes.

"No," Sabriel explained to him, "Kearu and Emerson will go with you."

Lautaro let out another sigh of relief, as he started to get his hopes up again that things may probably after all work in his favor this time before saying, "Oh thank you, thank you all!"

"I do not think I am in the right place mentally to do anything right now," said Emerson, her face showing hardly any emotional range at all, only sadness that she was keeping within herself was showcased across her face.

"Perhaps you guys should take Mist, I will

stay here keeping an eye on the train," she told them

as her voice lowered.

"Sure thing, Emerson," said Kearu, assuring

her, "You just stay here and rest, I will take Mist

and accompany Lautaro to the castle."

"Well now that everyone knows what to do,

let us get going," said Sabriel as he got up from his

seat and started hurrying to head out of the train's

compartment, to enter the locomotive, and exit out

towards his assigned task.

Just before he was about to leave the

compartment, he turned around to face his friends to

look at them one more time, but he especially

turned his attention towards Lautaro who gave him

a subtle awe stare, "You guys are amazing, never forget that I will meet you on the other end."

He then proceeded to head towards the locomotive to get off the train, as Lautaro felt a sense of melancholy at the fact that his friend Sabriel was out of sight. Though he knew that surely he would get to see him again eventually, the current moment felt to him like an approaching end of all his worries.

Emerson started heading towards the locomotive, as Lautaro, Kearu, and Mist followed after her, they all got up from their seats.

Once, the tenderhearted group of friends were all in the locomotive, they each knew it was time to say their farewells in the case that something went wrong and they would never get to see each other again.

"I wish you guys the infinite of best luck there could be," Emerson told them as she simultaneously hugged all of them, "I will be here waiting for you guys."

"No matter what happens, I will forever be grateful for what you guys have done to help me get here," Lautaro told his friends as they finished hugging each other.

"Stay safe," said Kearu to Emerson, "We will be back as soon as possible, hopefully with Lau's plane!"

He smiled at her, and got off the train, as Lautaro and Mist accompanied him. The trio started walking on the cobbler street heading towards the castle, as they turned around to wave goodbye at

Emerson one last time. Standing on the edge of the

locomotive's walking ledge, she waved goodbye

back at them as she gave them a tender smile,

nodding to them to continue on their quest.

"So what do you think," asked Kearu as they

walked down the street.

"About what," asked Lautaro.

"What's around you," said Kearu.

Realizing that his friend meant the central

kingdom, and noting the majestic, glossy robes that

the civilians were wearing in sharp shades of every

existent color to the human eye, Lautaro said, "It is

neat, beyond what I am used to back at home."

"Say you claim to not be from here," Kearu

asked him "Are you truly from another world?"

"I think so," said Lautaro as he continued,
"Everything I have seen is out of the ordinary."

"If what you are saying is true, then there
must be something that brought you here," Kearu
implied to him.

"Maybe so," said Lautaro quietly, unsure
what to respond exactly towards this statement.

"Hey check this out," said Kearu as he softly
nudged Lautaro in his left shoulder, he proceeded to
start walking over to a nearby water fountain that
had a statue of a female angel, who had sparkly
water coming out from her eyes, looking like tears.
She was standing in a position where she was
looking up at the sky, leading the tears, coming
from the side of her eyes to fall to solid hair, which
created beautiful trails of shining water along the

245

lines of her sculpted hair that would fall into the water fountain in the form of droplets.

"Such beautiful art," said Lautaro while inspecting the statue.

Kearu then pulled out a penny from his pocket and handed it to Lautaro, telling him, "Throw it in the fountain and make a wish."

Lautaro closely looked at the penny, it had an image of a fish with a slight colorful shine on it, he momentarily closed his eyes and wished to go back home in his mind as he threw the penny into the fountain. It was submerged into the fountain of the sparkly water, which Mist was drinking from hastily.

"Don't tell me what you wished for," Kearu

told him immediately, "but hopefully it becomes

true, now let us keep walking towards the castle."

Lautaro and Kearu walked up to the castle,

as Mist followed close behind them. It was guarded

by knights.

"State your business here," one of the

knights demanded of them.

"My friend here, Lautaro, wants to get his

plane back," said Kearu.

"The plane that was found is under the

kingdom's reign of investigation," one of the

knights angrily informed them.

"You do not understand," said Lautaro

shakily, "That is my plane and I am not from here, I

would like to get back home."

"Where are you exactly from," the knight asked him, raising his suspicions over what Lautaro's true intentions were.

"Umm," Lautaro immediately went into thinking mode as he remembered his background in which that for most of his life he was stateless until he had married into citizenship so he was always bound to be moving around, and therefore he felt no true alignment to any place, "Not from here that is for sure."

"We are going into isolation, are we not," chimed in Kearu, stepping in to speak up for Lautaro "So let him see the King so he can venture out of our kingdom at the very least."

The knights looked at them skeptical but decided to allow them in.

"Is the dog yours," they asked the two men.

"Yes, sir," said Lautaro.

One of the knights led Lautaro, Kearu, and Mist through the corridors of the castle. The inside of the castle was adorned in red, it appeared to be made out of some sort of red jewelry. The floors were plated in the shapes of diamonds of red and white tiles, which created a menacing welcome to all who stepped in of the castle. The knight brought them to where the King was along with his Queen, walking through a long corridor that was empty besides some walls having paintings of all who were and are part of royalty. Lautaro felt that the inside of the castle gave off a shallow vibrance.

Once in the royal room, the knight shut the door behind Lautaro, Kearu, and Mist as he left them alone with the royalty.

"Who despite requests of involute dare come see me," declared the king angrily.

"Umm yes, I need my plane back," Lautaro inquired.

"He is not from here and needs to get his plane to get back home," Kearu chimed in to speak up for Lautaro, who he could tell was incredibly nervous by the tone of his voice.

"Honey, must I say these gentlemen appear folie," said the Queen, who had blonde wavy hair and wore a crown made out of pure jewelry.

She appeared younger than the King, and Lautaro noticed that around her neck that she was wearing the necklace that the Bonaire grandmother

had given to him before he had set off to fly in the

Caribbean Sea. Whereas King Hansen was older,

and had a big grey beard, his crown was made of

hard metals adorned in soft material with small

jewelry on it.

"Hey that is my necklace," Lautaro

exclaimed, trying his best to remain calm.

"Is it," the queen said showing a slight

disgust at him as she held onto it with her hands to

inspect it more sharply, "I think not anymore."

Lautaro felt boiling mad, however, he dared

not say anything since he was aware of the risk of

the situation in which he was in.

"The plane we found, is it yours," asked the

King harshly.

"Yes, it is," said Lautaro, trying his best to not show any sort of emotions.

"What is your business here," King Hansen asked him cruelly.

"None, I just need to get back home," said Lautaro, as he was starting to get annoyed by how he now felt that he was being invasively interrogated.

"I do not believe in accidents, for all I know you could be a spy," yelled the King at him.

"Umm and why do you assume the worst of me," said Lautaro as he started to break off his cool demeanor, feeling provoked by the king's ridiculous accusations "I just need to get back home!"

"With all due respect, sir, Lautaro he is no harm to anyone, he just needs to get back home,"

Kearu stepped in to say in defense of his friend

before he would get any madder.

"And who are you," the King asked Kearu.

"Me? I am someone who decided to help

him," explained Kearu.

"Helping troubled people can get you in

trouble as well," said the King.

"Leave my castle now," the King demanded

of them as he stood up from his throne.

"I need my airplane back, though,"

interrupted Lautaro.

"Leave, or you will be executed," said the

King, briskly swaying one of his arms to express his

anger.

"Please spare my friend a chance," Kearu

started to plead.

"I see you two are choosing death, very well

then call in the guards, Lazuli," ordered the King.

Lazuli started calling in the knights who

soon surrounded the room. "GUARDS, GUARDS,

GUARDS, COME IN," she shouted brusquely.

Chapter 10:The Grendel and The Lone Baby

Emerson had been waiting for a while on the

locomotive, she was resting as she had been

mourning over the death of her grandparents. After

some long minutes had passed by, she went for a

walk in the streets to clear her mind. She got off the

train and made certain it was securely closed before

heading out to the streets. Exiting the train station,

she walked down the sedulous streets, pushing her

way through the busy crowds, she walked upon the

alleyways to the sides of the small shops instead as

they appeared to be more pleasant for the mind to

wonder.

She started walking upon an empty alley, it

was gloomy and trashy in the environment, but

peaceful in sound, good enough to give Emerson

time to process the recent events that had just

occurred.

As she walked past a trash container, she

thought she heard a whimper, however, she ignored

it as she thought it was just her imagination, or her

racing thoughts being sorted out. She kept walking,

and as she was about to turn the corner of the

alleyway into the principal streets again, a Grendel

stopped her.

"Say what would a lovely girl like you be doing around here," the Grendel asked her.

"Walking," she said, not knowing nor caring about The Grendel's motif to stop her in her tracks as her sadness was overbearing all of her thoughts.

"I think you should turn around," the Grendel told her, giving her a wickedly enormous grin, "there is something in need of protection."

"I do not know what you mean," said Emerson, confused and irritated by what he was telling her "I am taking a walk."

"You know things happen for a reason, go back and search for something," the Grendel insisted, his grin fading away, his menacing fangs, hiding away.

"You are kind of sure to be particular," said Emerson, noting his strange behavior, "But I guess I will look back."

"Very well," said Grendel, adjusting its coat on, "If you have the compassion to share, extend it to your findings."

"Okay," said Emerson, returning to walk back where she had come from, "What am I supposed to find?"

She turned around to face the Grendel, but he had gone out of sight, nowhere to be found. Tempted to leave and continue on her walk, but curious to know why the Grendel encountered her, she walked back from where she came back. As she passed by the trash container, she heard a slight movement coming from it. She realized that maybe something was in it.

She opened the trash container and saw a carton box laying on top of a dump of trash, something was moving in it. She opened the box and to her surprise saw it was a baby, a human baby, who started crying at the sight of her.

Emerson was both astounded and surprised but worried about the baby. She quickly took the baby out of the trash container, along with the blanket it had come in as it was naked and held it into her arms, comforting it.

"Now who would leave you in such a terrible place," said Emerson. She looked around the alley, wondering if the baby belonged to anyone nearby but no one was in sight.

It took her awhile to process the situation, but she realized that she needed to take care of the baby's needs immediately. So she started to head out of the alley and rushed back to the train to get her money to buy basic necessities for the baby, so she started to question her instinct to help this little human being. Was it because she is a caring person or because she actually wants to take care of the baby?

As Emerson got off of her train, she decided that the reason for her intentions were the latter and said to the baby who was curiously staring at her, not saying a word, "I will name you Laanor!"

Holding the baby carefully in her arms, she went on her way to the local shops, buying food, diapers, and blankets for Laanor.

Chapter 11:Mad Kingdom

Lautaro started becoming frightened. He felt that this would soon be the end for him, his struggles, his bittersweet symphony.

"Thank you for everything you have done," said Lautaro to Kearu, "I like you, and hope this could have turned out differently."

"I am not going down without a fight," said Kearu as he lifted his hands up getting ready to point them at the knights.

Just as he was about to release an energy beam of light, Lazuli pulled out a transparent, orange-rose colored wand made out of gemstones from her dress's pockets and she cast out a spell,

"Spessa" directed to trap Kearu in a crystal
blockade.

This shocked Kearu, "You are a gem person,
I thought your kind went extinct!"

"I am the last of my kind," said Lazuli,
continuing to say, "Adding in value to my marriage
to the King."

"Now, Lautaro, defenseless, and Kearu
enclosed by the jeweled capsule, along with Mist,
knew that their fates were no longer in their hands.

"I will give the honor of killing you to my
best knight," said King Hansen.

From the crowd of surrounding knights
emerged a knight who stood out, his armor of silver
with a black star rested on it, it was larger and had

bulkier edges than that of the armor that the other knights in the room bore.

He sauntered to the front of the room to face Lautaro and Kearu. When he took his mask off, he revealed himself to be Sabriel!

"Sabriel," cried out Lautaro as he jumped with joy, "I knew you would come to save us!"

"Actually," the King interrupted as he put one of his hands over Sabriel's shoulder, "Sabriel is my best knight, I sent him on a mission to bring you to me."

Lautaro felt his heart stop, as this shocked both him and Kearu in disbelief.

"How could you," said Lautaro, trying to hold back tears, and not show all the anger he was holding within himself.

"I wanted to trust you," said Kearu as he slammed his fists against the crystal glass case in which he was in.

"I-I am sorry, you guys," said Sabriel as he lowered his head, pulling out his sword from his side strap.

"What are you waiting for," shouted King Hansen as he got closer to the group, "Kill them now, Sabriel!"

"As you say, my King," said Sabriel, he raised his sword up pointing it at Lautaro, getting ready to kill him.

Lautaro crouched down, eyes closed, expecting for the worst to happen. However, Sabriel turned around with the sword in his hand, and instead impaled it onto the King's stomach.

Kearu, and Lautaro both gasped in surprise,

as the king said to Sabriel while blood started

coming out from the corner of his mouth, "You dare

end me, child, for I treated you like the son I never

had!"

He then fell to the ground, coughing up

blood and dying in despair. Once he let out his last

breath, Sabriel walked up to where King Hansen

layed on the ground, pulled out his sword and

reached for his crown.

He then continued on to crown himself

declaring, "From now and forward, I am everyone's

King, King Sabriel, with my newfound wife, Queen

Lazuli."

"Queen Lazuli then walked to where King

Sabriel stood and gave him a passionate kiss. All

the other knight men in the room started kneeling

down to show respect to their new leader, King

Sabriel.

Lautaro, still dumbfounded by the entire

situation, as he stood up, asked King Sabriel, "So

are we free to go, can I get my plane back?"

Kearu started sensing that something was

entirely off about Sabriel's character, so he

immediately started kicking and hitting on the

crystal jar that surrounded him to break free. It

started shattering, slowly, little by little. King

Sabriel and Queen Lazuli started walking back to

their thrones.

King Sabriel, along with his Queen, turned

around ominously to face Lautaro, before

replying, "About that Lautaro, you have no value to

me or our society, along with your friends,

Knightmen execute them!"

Lautaro, horrified by this betrayal, started

backing up against the large, gemstone jar in which

Kearu and Mist were entrapped in.

The knights all started closing in on them, as

King Sabriel and Queen Lazuli watched in

amusement the entire situation. Lautaro

immediately started helping Kearu shatter the

crystal case break as he pounded his fists and

started kicking against it.

"Come on Mist, use your fog," Kearu yelled

at the dog who was pouncing erratically against the

crystal jar.

Lautaro started noticing a small, fog cape

surrounding him and Kearu, as the gem jar finally

started breaking. The knights were about to swing at Lautaro their swords when suddenly Lautaro's vision was blurred by complete, grey thick fog clouds!

For a moment, for Lautaro all he could see was grey fog surrounding him, it was as if he was in a pure fog-scape realm, then he turned around and saw Kearu and Mist right next to him.

"What is this," Lautaro asked Kearu, "Any longer in this world and I think I might depersonalize!"

"Oh do not worry, this is Mist's power, he is teleporting us to safe ground."

The dark, grey fog slowly started fading away, and it appeared that Lautaro, Kearu, and Mist had arrived at where the water fountain of the angelic, crying woman was.

"Huh," said Lautaro, "we are back here."

"And by good luck," said Kearu as he reached for Lautaro's hand, "Come on, let us go!"

Kearu started leading Lautaro through the town's crowd, as Mist ran behind them back to the train. Once there, they were surprised to see Emerson with a baby.

"Woah Emerson, you didn't tell us you had a child," exclaimed Lautaro!

"I didn't, I adopted him," she said.

"Em, a baby is an incredibly large responsibility, you sure that you can handle this," Kearu asked her.

"If I've taken care of you guys during this journey, then I can take care of anyone I want to," exclaimed Emerson.

"Good enough," said Kearu," However we better get going now!"

"Why," Emerson asked him, "And did Lautaro get his plane back?"

"No he did not, Sabriel- he betrayed us," explained Kearu, "We are now declared enemies to the Kingdom, we are to be prosecuted!"

"Oh no, this is not good at all," said Emerson.

Lautaro, Kearu, and Emerson holding baby Laanor in her arms, all then hurried to get on the train locomotive, along with Mist.

"Kearu, may you take care of Laanor for me," said Emerson as she gently gave the sleeping baby to him.

"Aww," said Kearu at the sight of such a baby, "I guess I can be your uncle from now and on!"

He walked to the train's main compartment, getting buckled up and secured. Lautaro came in, he was noticeably sad as he took a seat next to Kearu who reached out his hand towards him, and reaffirmed him by telling him, "Do not worry, we got each other's backs now."

"Get ready, everyone," Emerson called out into the train's speakers.

The train took a turn around and immediately it started speeding back to where it had come from. They entered the tunnel of darkness that leads to the rocky, mountainous area.

Meanwhile, back in the castle of Alnidor, King Sabriel and Queen Lazuli are having a discourse with their knight men.

"Should we send troops to get them," one of the knights asked them.

"No, not yet, however, make sure to place these dissidents on the terrorist list," he ordered them.

"My king, they are heading back towards the rocky valley, they are on the escape," another knight told them.

"Is that so," asked Sabriel "Lazuli, communicate with the rock Minotaur, activating him to annihilate them."

Lazuli, the last of her kind, a gem person is able to communicate and insert motifs into any of the rock, mineral, and gemstone elements using her magic. Utilizing her wand, she cast a spell out, "alexandrite!"

This spell shot out, and traveled all the way to the mountainous region surrounding the kingdom to insert murderous energy into the rock Minotaur...Emerson was conducting the train, they entered the rocky valley, "Not him again," she thought as the Minotaur started awakening, its' figure emerging from the mountainous rocks.

The rock Minotaur's eyes glowed red this time, illuminating that color within the lines on its body. It wielded not one, but two axes this time, hitting them down upon the ground, causing the ground to start breaking apart into an "X" shape.

The ground started trembling as it started breaking

apart, making it harder for Emerson to manage the

train among the bumpy ground. She started steering

the train to the center of the materializing

"X"-shaped fissure on the ground, as that is where

the gap is the smallest.

To better keep the baby safe, Kearu put baby

Laanor inside his shirt behind the buckled belt,

while firmly, but gently holding onto him. Lautaro

who was seated next to him did the same to Mist, he

and Kearu then held onto each other in a tight,

embracing hug, to keep a firm balance as the train

rampaged through bumpy grounds. Emerson started

nearing the center of the "X" as that is where the

opening gap is the smallest! She sped the train to go

its full speed, barely managing to get a hold unto the other side, as the gap started widening, the end trail of the train started to submerge in the train, Emerson kept pulling full speed of the train, managing to pull it out and into the land completely. They were safe for now, as the train continued on its way through the rocky valley until the dry land became green.

The rock Minotaur declared ,"Danger is but an illusion", before submerging back into the Rocky Mountains.

The group arrived at the evergreen mountains. By now it was nighttime. Emerson put the train to a stop, as she went from the locomotive to the main compartment to meet up with Lautaro, Kearu, Mist, and baby Laanor.

"Well we are safe for now," said Emerson," and how is Lannor doing?"

"He's sleeping," said Kearu as she showed her the baby.

"How adorable," said Emerson as she reached out to hold the baby from Kearu, tears of melancholia started rolling from her eyes, "He is so adorable and innocent, I will proudly take care of him."

"You are a wonderful woman," Kearu told her, "You have a lot of love to share, and that is truly special."

"Now what," Lautaro chimed to ask them, "What is going to happen to me?"

"Well, we cannot stay here for too long," said Kearu, "We need to leave Alnidor immediately."

"Why," Lautaro asked him. "If we were considered a threat when Hansen ruled, then we are even more so now that Sabriel is king," Kearu explained to him.

"Sabriel is king," said Emerson, shocked at this realization, "Wow, he sure did us dirty!"

"Yup," said Kearu, while pointing his attention to Mist, "Either way we need to get out of here."

"Wait," Emerson said, "I would at least like to say goodbye to my family...and...give them some news."

"That is fine," Kearu assured her. Emerson then walked over to where Mist was laying on the ground, she kneeled down to get closer to him.

"Mist, you know what to do, can you take us back to my town, where mom and dad are," she asked him as she began to pet him on the head with one of her hands while holding Laanor unto the other.

The dog began to wag its tail and suddenly clouds started appearing outside of the train's windows until the view of anything else was completely fogged up. Emerson got up and headed over to where Lautaro and Kearu were to take a seat with them. Lautaro who was amused by Mist's teleportation powers wondered if he could utilize them to get back home. The blurry fog started clearing from the windows, revealing a new view, they were now in the train station of Emerson's hometown.

Kearu, Lautaro, and Emerson holding baby Laanor got off the train as Mist followed them and they started walking towards her home. As they walked on the cobbler street, Lautaro felt that something was off, it took him a minute to realize that the streets were completely dark.

Chapter 12:Flower Petals

"Why are the streets so dark," Lautaro asked his colleagues, as he looked all around in total darkness at the streets which were only lit by the moons.

"The light, energy sources have been turned off by Sabriel and his army," explained Kearu to him before continuing on to explain, "as a demonstration of what further disobedience from the people can lead to."

"Well, that is terrible," said Lautaro, letting out a lowly sigh.

"It is," Kearu replied.

Once they reached Emerson's home, she knocked on the front door, and her family came out, they were all holding candles to light up their surroundings.

"Emerson, where have you been," her dad yelled out as he rushed to give her a hug.

He noticed the baby she was holding in her arms and surprised by this, he exclaimed,

"Emerson! Is that your child, don't tell me you and

one of the boy-"

"Dad, do not worry, it is my son but I

adopted him, saved him from neglect," Emerson

exclaimed attempting to ease down her father's

erroneous thoughts.

"Emerson, are you sure you can handle a

child," her mother chimed in to ask.

"Can I see," one of her siblings asked her.

"Yes you may," Emerson replied to her

brother as she turned her attention to her mother,

"Do not worry, mother, if I went on a dangerous

journey supervising grown men then I can take care

of anybody!"

"Well I hope you know what you are
doing," her mother said, "Now come inside we'll
continue talking."

"Actually...I can not do that," Emerson said,
"I am under prosecution, I have to leave the
kingdom."

"Oh no, do not tell me, you got in some
major trouble," her father exasperated.

"It is a lengthy story," Emerson said while
looking at her family, "the kingdom also killed
grandma and grandpa"

She started bursting into tears, remembering
the tragic fate that her grandparents had suffered.

"No, no, no," her father started wailing, "no,
this can not be!"

Lautaro and Kearu having watched the

family break into full sorrow during their discourse

from a distance knew that it would be best to give

them some personal time to discuss their matters, so

they walked out of the family's driveway and into

the empty street. Mist noticed this and followed

them behind.

The two remained quiet, Lautaro looked at

Mist, who was nearby as he approached the dog to

crouch down. "Hey fella, do you think you could

take me back to my world," he asked him.

Mist, the dog started to wag its tail, Lautaro

started tearing up, he wanted to go back home but

he knew that decision was out of his control.

"Agreeable boy," Lautaro said as he petted

Mist and got up.

Lautaro headed over to catch up to where Kearu was standing, he was looking up at the sky at the two moons.

"You know," Kearu said, "I sometimes feel like peace will never be achievable, however, one must always have hope for a better tomorrow."

"I definitely agree with you," Lautaro told him, "Even in my world, planet earth, I was stateless for most of my life which systematically imprisoned me from reaching my full potential, I would get angry and depressed at times, but I always kept hope to keep going."

"It seems to be a sentient's nature, no," Kearu asked him," However the human spirit should never be undermined, our minds itself are vibrational machines."

"What do you mean by that," Lautaro asked him, facing him with a curious flare.

"I will show you," Kearu told him as he walked a bit away from Lautaro to give himself enough personal space to move his arms around.

"Where there is light, there is hope," he exclaimed.

Suddenly, Kearu closed his eyes as he started to extend his arms out and move them about in front of himself in such a smooth manner as orbs of light started emerging all around him, he started glowing a bright yellow as his long hair which was tied up unloosened itself.

He put both of his arms out to his sides, as the bracelets on his arms started twirling around. The light orbs surrounding him started accumulating into the sky, levitating above him, forming a giant ball of light that started to slowly illuminate the entire kingdom.

This ball of light then proceeded to explode into a million sparks all across the kingdom, and as it rained down, it would merge where light sources would normally be, brightening up the entirety of the kingdom's light system once again.

Kearu then slowly put his arms down to his sides, and his glowing essence slowly faded away, as he opened his eyes.

"Woah, where did you learn to do that," Lautaro asked him, extremely amused by such fantastical performance.

"I really do not know exactly, it just comes naturally to me," Kearu explained trying to regain control of his rushing thoughts, "I had an extremely rough life, I felt I had to become my own light."

Lautaro ran up to him to hug him telling him, "I know what hurt is like, I know what it is to be human."

As they hugged each other in ever endearing, supportive silence, they heard Emerson and her family walk over to where they were.

"Kearu, what did you just do," Emerson asked, captivated by what she had just witnessed "We watched you do your thing and next thing we knew, the entire kingdom has been lit back up!"

"Yeah, a little light to keep hopes up," said Kearu as his goofy smile surfaced from his face for the first time in a while.

At that moment, Emerson's momentary happiness turned to full anxiety as she realized that she and her friends really needed to evacuate the kingdom immediately.

"Mom and Dad, I love you all so much," she said, tearing up.

"I love you all, all of you, my family," She said as she started crying nonstop.

Her mom who was carrying Laanor in her arms handed him over to her, "Take care of him, the love you have shown us, reign it over him," she stated as Emerson took him in his arms.

Emerson looked at her mother in tears, as she hugged her, her father joined in and so did her siblings, they all gave Emerson one huge, final embracing hug.

"Take care, my little conductor," her father told her.

They let go of Emerson as she kneeled down to say a final goodbye to her youngest sibling, Dey, who was only 5 years old, "Words cannot describe how much I will miss you, hopefully, we will see each other again someday," she declared as she hugged him.

She got up, and in tears started waving goodbye to her family as she, Lautaro, Kearu, and Mist began walking down the street...at last when her family was out of sight, she stopped waving.

Lautaro, Kearu, and Emerson holding Laanor in her arms started to speed walk down the cobbled street, as Mist ran closely behind them on his four legs.

As they passed by the streets, Lautaro admired the decorative street lamps lighting the way to the street station.

"You truly are a beautiful human," he exclaimed to Kearu, realizing that he was the reason for the lights to come up.

"Thank you," Kearu told him, letting out a flattering laugh, "I try my best!"

Once the group of friends had reached the train station, they hurried to run and get into Emerson's train, she started managing the locomotive as she handed Laanor over to Kearu, "keep an eye on the little one," she told him, as she made direct eye contact with him, signaling to him that she was serious about Laanor's well-being.

"Will do," said Kearu as he tightly held Laanor with one of his arms, to salute her with his other arm. Lautaro headed to the train locomotive, alongside Mist who was excitedly running in all directions, once onboard.

Lautaro reached out to grab Mist in his arms, as he followed Kearu who was holding Laanor into one of the train's compartments. Once there, they buckled up tightly. Emerson started the train engine, which let out a mighty roar, she started speeding the train up, faster than usual, to navigate it towards the nearest entry point into the neighboring kingdom, Poloram.

After the train had passed by an endless row of desolate woods, the train started to approach Poloram, which Emerson noticed that there was some sort of wooden barrier there that was being held up by two trees to the sides as they got closer. She started to speed up her train faster crashing into it, not caring for any damage done to the entry point and behold, they were now in Poloram!

The railroad track in which the train was on led down a slope that was entirely covered in a field of corn poppy flowers, the train passed right through it before Emerson decided to put it to a steady halt. She concluded that they were now safe to at the very least relax momentarily.

She unbuckled herself from the conductor's seat and exited the locomotive to head into the next section of the train to announce personally to Kearu and Lautaro that they had reached the kingdom of Poloram.

After hearing the news, Kearu, Lautaro, both

got excited as they immediately unbuckled

themselves to get up from their seats. Lautaro, who

had been carrying Mist, let go of him so he could

freely roam around. Kearu, then went up to gently

hand the baby over to Emerson in her arms. The

baby was starting to wake up and open its tiny eyes.

"Awww," Emerson exclaimed before

assuring the baby, "Do not worry, you are safe with

mommy and your uncles now."

Lautaro joyfully chuckled as Emerson now

considered him close enough to be an uncle for her

child.

The group of friends decided to get off the

train for a break and catch a view of the spectacular

corn poppy flower fields. As the group of friends all

got off the train via the locomotive's slider doors, the sun began to emerge.

Emerson while holding Laanor firmly in one hand, and holding onto a rail with the other to get off the train exclaimed "The sun, it is so bright and beautiful, yet it does it all alone!"

As she got off the train she continued on to say with heartened tears, "we have relief from danger now, however it makes me sad to think of all the voices that have been silenced and lights that have been turned off unknowingly."

Kearu who had been looking up at the petals floating, flowing through the breezy morning wind stated, responded to what she said, "I like to think of all empowered individuals who met an untimely demise to be like flower petals in the sky, always flowing about until they become one with nature then the universe."

He then turned his attention to Lautaro who was standing still, admiring the sun. Mist had begun to run around the fields playfully. Lautaro, while sad at the thought that he may never be able to return to his world, realized that he had to be grateful that he was still alive and had met some highly noble people along his journey, something he found to be a rarity.

"You know what I think about all this," Lautaro said as he got closer to where Kearu and Emerson holding baby Laanor were standing, as he embraced them all with his arms bringing them closer to where he was footing to tell them, "It is an extreme rarity we even met, for that, I say that we will only ever need each other, for it seems anybody

can be my world!"

Made in the USA
Monee, IL
27 June 2021

72447503R00173